Eternal City
A medieval fiction novel about politics and intrigue in an ancient city
Marina Pacheco

Marina Pacheco

contents

Offer		V
1.	Chapter 1	1
2.	Chapter 2	11
3.	Chapter 3	17
4.	Chapter 4	29
5.	Chapter 5	42
6.	Chapter 6	55
7.	Chapter 7	64
8.	Chapter 8	74
9.	Chapter 9	79
10.	Chapter 10	98
11.	Chapter 11	112
12.	Chapter 12	123
13.	Chapter 13	133
14.	Chapter 14	138

15.	Chapter 15	142
16.	Chapter 16	154
17.	Chapter 17	164
18.	Chapter 18	168
19.	Chapter 19	179
20.	Chapter 20	184
21.	Chapter 21	190
Get all my short stories for FREE!		214
Also By		215
About Author		220

Sign up for Marina Pacheco's no-spam newsletter that only goes out when there is a new book or freebie available and get a whole load of freebies!

Details can be found at the end of this book.

Chapter 1

Galen and Alcuin sat on a low wall in the shadows of a ruined tower in Rome, waiting for Carbo. Judging by the position of the sickle moon high above them in a cloudless sky, Galen estimated it had been at least two hours since the big monk had gone off with the injured Bartolo. The thought of that monk pricked Galen's conscience for not even attempting to help him.

Over and over again, Galen had to remind himself of what Bartolo had done. He'd betrayed Marozia and literally stabbed her in the back. He may have been acting upon the orders of a higher power, but he'd broken the rules of God.

God decreed thou shalt not kill. The Benedictine order ruled that no monk should draw blood. Another stab of conscience, for Galen had also drawn blood. In self-defence, but blood nonetheless.

He wanted to ask Alcuin for his thoughts on the matter, but was hesitating. This wasn't the best time or place. They had been warned that the streets of Rome were dangerous come nightfall, so it was best to remain hidden and silent.

Besides, his legs felt shaky and his guts throbbed with pain, while Alcuin looked pale and strained. Not surprising after their day of death and flight when Alcuin had supported Galen most of the way to Rome. Galen wished he could do something to put his friend's mind at ease, but, in his own tired stupor and feeling as shaken as he was, nothing helpful came to mind.

The chill wind strengthened, reminding Galen that winter was on the way, and he pulled his cloak tighter about himself, wrapping his fingers into the warm wool.

'Are you alright?' Alcuin whispered into his ear.

Galen nodded and patted Alcuin's arm, his hand still wrapped in the cloak.

'Where is that damned Carbo?' Alcuin mumbled more to himself than to Galen.

Alcuin was usually the calm, contented one, so his irritation confirmed that he was in a state of emotional upheaval. It was Galen's usual condition, so perhaps he was less shaken now than Alcuin. Or maybe he was just too tired and distracted by pain to think or feel anything.

'What should we do, Galen?' Alcuin murmured.

The question surprised Galen, who was more used to following than being asked for advice. Although it wasn't unheard of from Alcuin, maybe the miracle made him even more likely to ask for Galen's opinion.

'What should we do about what?' Galen asked, keeping his voice low as well.

'About the pope. Brother Bartolo said Marozia was killed upon his orders. That's difficult to accept, but if it's true... What manner of man does that make the pope?'

It was the same question Galen had been asking himself.

'A political one, but we always knew that. I would have been more accepting of their actions if they'd tried to stop Marozia or put her on trial. But they expunged her and her followers from existence. Like they knew what they were doing was wrong and they tried to hide it.'

'It looks like a crime,' Alcuin said, then tilted his head, for there were voices coming from nearby.

A group of drunks were wending their way down a nearby path, one singing off-key, his raucous voice occasionally obscured by the loud shushes of his companions.

'If the pope knew he was in the wrong,' Alcuin said, as the men's voices grew distant and then faded away, 'and did it anyway, I worry about his trustworthiness.'

'But we must remember that we only have Bartolo's word that he was acting upon the pope's orders.'

'He didn't seem like he was lying.'

'He believed what he was saying, but he never said that the pope ordered him directly. I wish I had noticed that earlier and asked about it. For all we know, somebody else manipulated Bartolo.'

'Either way,' Alcuin said, 'it makes me less keen to meet the pope. I'm not sure I would trust his judgement.'

Galen nodded because, once again, he and Alcuin were of the same mind.

'I wish we could discover the truth, but I fear that will be beyond us and our meagre connections and abilities.'

'And far too dangerous. You, me, Carbo and Bartolo were the only survivors of the massacre. I fear we would be killed if any of us ever mention what we saw. Which makes me feel like the sooner we leave Rome, the better.'

Galen was inclined to agree. But after deciding that he should speak to the pope, for whatever truths it might reveal, he wasn't ready to give up on the plan.

'Maybe we should find out what we can about the pope before we decide either way.'

'I suppose that would be the most sensible decision. Otherwise our arrival and sudden departure from Rome might also occasion comment.'

Galen doubted anyone would notice their existence, but Alcuin always ascribed more importance to the two of them, so he just nodded.

'Drat, really!' Alcuin snapped, making Galen jump. 'Where is that damned Carbo? At this rate, we'll freeze to death.'

At that moment a large shadow came shuffling towards them, walking slowly, and Galen held his breath. Was this a robber? Would a bandit be walking the streets alone?

'Brother Galen? Brother Alcuin?'

It was Carbo's hesitant voice.

'About time!' Alcuin said and stood up.

'Sorry,' Carbo said, keeping his voice low. 'I got lost. I feared I'd never find you again.'

Alcuin took a deep breath, as if gearing up for a ticking off, then his shoulders slumped.

'It's a big city. Will you be able to find the abbey?'

'I've been to San Agato before and we stayed a while, so I know the route from the city gate to the abbey.'

'Will they let us in at this hour?' Alcuin asked as he helped Galen to his feet.

Sitting in the cold night air had chilled Galen's muscles to the point where he could barely hobble and every step was painful. He wrapped his cloak more tightly about himself and tried not to slow Alcuin and Carbo as they started down the dark streets.

At least Carbo only had to stop once to ask for directions from a pair of guards standing before a solid oak and iron-bound door lit by a flaming torch.

As they left the guards behind, going in the direction they had pointed, Carbo said, 'I only hope his friend Fra' Martinus is still abbot there.'

'Why might he not be?'

Galen really didn't want to have to travel further if the abbot had changed. He'd have to be carried at this rate, and the thought of having to go elsewhere stung his eyes with tears.

'Who knows what may happen to a person? The last time we visited was ten years ago.'

'They wouldn't turn us away, though, would they?' Alcuin said. 'I mean, we're still travellers in need of somewhere safe to spend the night.'

'True enough, but without Fra' Martinus, we might not get much help beyond somewhere to stay. Whereas, if it is still Fra' Arnal's friend in charge, he may be able to get you to see the pope.'

'Well then, let us hope he is still the abbot. But right now, all I really care about is a bed.'

Just as Galen was worried that he'd collapse before they got to the abbey, Carbo stopped before a well-fortified door. This one had a dim lamp fluttering at the entrance that illuminated an iron chain with a stirrup-like handle.

'This is it.'

Carbo pulled the chain which set a bell clanking within. Galen wished they'd arrived during daylight hours. All he could see now were the looming shadows of tightly packed buildings, tighter than Lundenburh and far taller.

Nothing came from the pulling of the bell and Galen found himself mesmerised by the dim lamp flame, protected as it was from the wind by a shield of smoke-blackened glass. Carbo gave an impatient tut and pulled the chain several times with more force.

The bell clanked so loudly now that Galen was sure it would wake the entire abbey. But it still felt like an awfully long time before a section of wood was slid aside from the grille in the middle of the door and they were glared at by a dark pair of eyes.

'What is the meaning of this racket?' the porter asked. 'If you are pilgrims, you should go to the Diaconiae in Borgo.'

'Do we look like pilgrims?' Carbo asked, his voice getting louder in his irritation.

'Yes, you do.'

'Well, we aren't. And I must see your abbot.'

'Everyone is at Compline, so you'll have to wait to see the abbot. Although why you should see him, I don't know. We provide beds for many pilgrims to the city. They don't all demand, or get to see, our abbot.'

'I have a message from an old friend. If your abbot is still Fra' Martinus,' Carbo said and reached into his habit to pull out a letter and wave it at the grille.

'Fra' Martinus is still our abbot,' the porter said, his expression becoming less uncompromising at the mention of his abbot's name.

At the same time, a key was pushed into the substantial lock. It turned with a loud clack. Then the door was pulled back by the grey-haired, but powerfully built porter holding an iron-studded club in one hand.

'Well, it's a relief that the abbot is still around,' Carbo said with a big grin as he forced his way inside, making a gap wide enough for Alcuin to help Galen in. 'Then we will wait where you want until Fra' Martinus can see us.'

The interior of the abbey was only marginally better lit than the road outside. An oil lamp illuminated a moderately sized reception room with a high ceiling, an indistinct fresco on the far wall and a long bench beside the door. It was too dark to make out much else in the flickering light.

'Wait here. I'll fetch Brother Francesco, our terrier. He'll sort out your accommodation.'

'And what of the abbot?'

'Do you know nothing of patience? You may have to wait until the morning before you see him. In the meantime you can give me your letter. I'll make sure our fra' gets it.'

Carbo looked undecided for a moment, but officialdom awed him, and it didn't surprise Galen when he handed over the letter.

'Make sure it is delivered into the fra's hands.'

'What do you take us for?'

The porter spoke in a belligerent tone and added a gesture that Galen suspected was rude, but there was no time for a riposte as the porter hurried away.

'At least we're in,' Carbo said.

'That is a relief,' Alcuin said as he guided Galen to the bench and helped him to sit.

Through the half-ajar door, the little group could see the porter having a low-voiced conversation with a monk who glanced briefly at the huddle of Galen and Alcuin, then at Carbo, standing beside the door, before he hurried away. The porter came back to them but said nothing.

'Dear God, are we to sit here all night?' Carbo asked.

'You asked to see our abbot. You must now be patient.'

'I would wait till the end of time itself, but one of our number is not as robust as I am and is in need of a bowl of something sustaining to eat and a place to sleep.'

'I'm alright,' Galen said softly.

'That's good of you to say, Brother Galen,' Carbo said as he placed a rather too heavy hand on Galen's shoulder. 'But I don't see why you should wait. We would never treat a traveller in this shabby way at home, but clearly hospitality is different in this proud city.'

'We have a lot more pilgrims to contend with,' the porter said.

'We may have fewer, but believe me, you'd be glad to see our monastery in your travels because there are no other places that can offer you sanctuary. Whilst in Rome, there are plenty of other options.'

'You can always try one of the others.'

'After I have spoken to your fra' I might just do that!' Carbo said, his voice growing increasingly loud.

'Carbo, it's alright, I can wait,' Galen said and laid his hand over the big man's.

'No, it isn't alright. But if you don't like it, I won't make a scene.'

At that moment, a dark, hunchbacked man appeared.

'I am Brother Francesco, the terrier. Are these our guests, Brother Donato?' he asked, straining to raise his head as he looked up at the porter and the travellers.

It was the first time they'd heard the porter's name and Galen found himself agreeing with Carbo that Roman monks were less than friendly.

'This way please, brothers,' the old monk said. He didn't wait to see whether he was being followed.

They were led to a surprisingly small dormitory that held around forty beds, two thirds of which were occupied by pilgrims. Some were already curled up in bed, the rest chatted as they prepared for the night.

'We'll take that spot,' Carbo said, before the terrier could speak. 'Brother Galen can have the corner bed.'

'Also, would it be possible to arrange some hot water for tea,' Alcuin said.

Brother Francesco gave an exaggerated sigh and pointed with his thumb. 'The kitchen is over there. If you're lucky some of the staff may still be working.'

'Thank you,' Alcuin said and started digging in their now-rather-empty bag for the tea when a very young monk, most likely newly ordained, came running and bowed as he arrived.

'I am Brother Piero, Fra' Martinus's assistant. He will see the brother with the message for him now. Please follow me.'

'About time,' Carbo muttered. 'I won't be long.'

'I'll go too,' Alcuin said.

Galen could understand why he wanted to go; such an important meeting would need diplomacy. They'd also both feel more comfortable if Alcuin could see the abbot with his own eyes and get a sense of the reliability of the man and the safety of the abbey.

'But who will look after Brother Galen?' Carbo asked.

'I'll be fine,' Galen said, trying to keep his expression confident even though a part of him was terrified of being left alone amongst strangers.

CHAPTER 2

A slamming door startled Galen. He'd drifted off to sleep and woke curled up on the bed, dawn light spilling in through the dormitory door. Had he been so exhausted he'd drifted off while waiting for Alcuin and Carbo?

With a start he looked around for the two men.

'Relax, Brother, Alcuin just went off to relieve himself,' Carbo said from where he was seated at the end of his bed.

'Ah,' Galen said and shrank down into the shadows, then clenched his fists and sat up as straight as he could. So much for his resolve to be braver.

Despite his exhaustion, or perhaps because of it and the pain, Galen rarely slept well, so he must have been extremely tired to have slept through the night, and that in the pilgrim's dormitory filled with people he didn't know.

Maybe it was because he knew he'd be protected by Alcuin and Carbo. Galen was grateful for that, and for the fact that Alcuin did it as a matter of course. But it also made him ashamed that he couldn't look after himself or overcome his fears. Chief amongst those being what had happened at the meeting with the abbot.

'What did the abbot say?' Galen asked Carbo.

'That he wants to see you.'

That made Galen's heart kick with fright.

'But I don't know him.'

'If you want to see the pope, you'll have to talk to him.'

'I'm afraid he's right,' Alcuin said as he arrived, a mug of steaming tea in his hand.

'Why must I see him?'

'Because he is curious about you and, as he told us, many people want to see the pope. Unless you have a sponsor, you'll never get in.'

'When?' Galen said, almost bereft of breath as his fear mounted.

'When he calls,' Alcuin said.

Now Galen was glad that it was Prime and he could make his way with the pilgrims into the church for the first prayers of the day. It was dark inside and the candles did little to provide illumination, but it impressed Galen nonetheless. The stone edifice was as large as Lundenburh's cathedral, yet it was only the church of an abbey.

The monks took up their positions in the choir; the pilgrims and other visitors clustered around the back of the church. Galen and his companions landed up standing to the far left, so tightly crowded about by the whispering people that they were pressed against the wall. It was cold but had the virtue of keeping Galen propped up. While he waited for the service to begin he noticed that the floor was paved with long flat stones that had names and dates engraved into them.

'Gravestones?' Galen mouthed to Alcuin.

Alcuin gave an expressive half shrug, half nod and pointed behind himself at the wall that had been carved out to provide yet more burial space. Maybe that explained the heavy use of incense that didn't quite cover the stink. Until then, Galen had assumed the smell came from the pilgrims.

The murmurs of the congregation ceased as the monks started their chant. Galen lowered his head and focused on the prayers rising to heaven on the incense smoke that drifted into the rafters, carried by the hundreds of voices that filled the dark space and echoed off the stone.

Galen was grateful to be in the presence of holy men and thanked God that he and Alcuin had made it this far. He prayed he'd see the pope and head home as soon as possible. Finally, he asked God to keep his family safe.

After the prayers, Alcuin, Galen and Carbo followed the now-rowdy pilgrims back outside. After weeks of sleeping outdoors it was strange to be so hemmed in with towering stone and reddish brick walls. So Galen sighed with relief to see the cloud-streaked sky as they emerged into the courtyard. A clatter of wings drew his attention to a squat, circular tower with hundreds of tiny entrances filled with pigeons.

'Look at the size of that pigeon coop. Even the way the Romans farm pigeons is on another level.' Then Galen tilted his head all the way back and said, 'And this bell tower. Have you ever seen anything like it?'

'Never,' Alcuin said. 'When we approached Rome, we saw so many towers it seemed like the city was a stone forest more than the abode of man. But since we arrived in the dark, I didn't realise the scale of the towers. It feels like we could touch heaven from such a height.'

Galen realised that he and Alcuin were blocking the pilgrims from leaving the church, and they might have pushed their way out but for Carbo's strategically placed bulk. Galen stepped sideways and the people made haste to the pilgrims' kitchen for breakfast.

'I would rather have gone with the monks,' Alcuin said, watching as an old man shoved his way through the crowd gathered around a large cauldron.

'Get back, you,' Carbo snapped to another pair, rushing to the two lay brothers who were doling out ladlefuls of a thin pottage accompanied by a slice of bread. 'I'll get our food. There's no need for you to fight your way to the front, Brother Galen.'

It looked more like a melee than an orderly queue and Galen was grateful he wouldn't have to compete in it. Carbo merely waded through everyone like they weren't there.

'I need to tell you something,' Alcuin murmured and drew Galen further away from the crowd. 'We had to tell Fra' Martinus about what happened on the road, the dream, you know, and how it played out.'

'You told him? We decided to keep our connection to that woman a secret.'

'He wasn't inclined to help so we had no choice. Just be aware of it when you go to see him.'

It made Galen even more nervous but, if Alcuin had decided it was necessary, he accepted that. So he nodded and checked on Carbo.

Carbo was having a heated argument with the serving lay brother who seemed to be saying he could only take one bowl. But after some vigorous pointing towards Galen and Alcuin, he emerged victorious, balancing three bowls.

'Thanks, Carbo,' Alcuin said as they settled on a stone bench that encircled the narrow courtyard and gave them some pleasantly warming sun.

'I hope the monks eat better than this,' Carbo said gloomily, scooping up what looked more like a soup than a decently thick pottage.

'I'm sure they do,' Alcuin said, keeping his tone bright.

Galen didn't mind. Anything more than this would sit like an indigestible ball in his stomach.

Once the pilgrims had eaten their meal, they wrapped up their meagre possessions and left to visit the holy sites of Rome.

'Apparently they aren't allowed to stay,' Carbo said in a stage whisper. 'You can only have a bed during the day if you're ill.'

'That's probably why they give them a meal so early,' Alcuin said.

Galen nodded. Usually, monks only had one meal in winter, in the middle of the day after Sext. In the summer that was supplemented with a light supper after Vespers.

'What of us, then?' Galen asked. 'Will we have to leave too?'

'We were told to wait, so that's what we'll do,' Alcuin said. 'In the meantime, you need to rest. Once the kitchens are clear I'll get some hot water and make you one of your uncle's teas.'

'I'm surprised you still have them,' Galen said, relieved that he would get something to alleviate both his pain and fatigue.

'Well... not your uncle's,' Alcuin said, 'but the same things. First from the king's leech, then Hatim, and lastly from Carbo's monastery. I'll have a word with the infirmarius here sometime, although your uncle's letter on your treatment is getting pretty dog-eared.'

Galen nodded and murmured, 'As long as you don't mention the rest.'

Long ago he'd wondered what it might be like to live in a monastery where nobody knew about his black past. It was strange that he was about to find out, and in a far more distant monastery than he could ever have imagined.

Chapter 3

T hree hours later, when Galen and his companions were leaving the church after Terce, the call, delivered by young Brother Piero, finally came. Galen bundled up his courage and, accompanied by Alcuin and Carbo, made his way to the abbot's room.

'The fra' only wishes to see Brother Galen,' Piero said, looking uncertainly up at Alcuin and Carbo, both of whom towered over him.

'We'll wait outside the fra's room,' Alcuin said, giving Piero a nod to say they had heard him, but equally, he was going to be ignored. 'If you need help, Galen, just shout and we'll come running.'

Galen couldn't imagine what a sick old man might do to him, although he was an authority figure, which always frightened Galen. He nodded, trying to look capable, then took a shaky breath and tapped at the abbot's door.

Alcuin had given Galen a detailed description of the man and his room, so neither came as a surprise. Galen seldom met people who were more frail than himself, but considering Fra' Martinus's gaunt face, Galen could understand why he hadn't been attending the daily offices.

A long-haired servant had just helped Fra' Martinus to sit upright in his bed and was still pulling the blanket back into place. He turned to look Galen up and down in an appraising way that felt nothing like a servant — they normally kept their head bowed and their gaze averted.

'My physician,' Fra' Martinus said in the soft, scratchy voice of the old. 'Master Venerio is the best in Rome, so all the most desperate call for his aid.'

'Oh, I see.'

Now the man's attitude and his stained apron made more sense.

'You are ill too,' the physician said as a matter of fact, rather than a question.

Galen took a step back. His experience of healers was mixed at best and he didn't want to be pushed into anything he'd find difficult to refuse.

'I have been told there is nothing more that can be done for me.'

'Doubtless some quack told you that. What was his name?'

'I doubt you would have heard of him,' Galen said, praying this would stop the man who had the zealous look of an intrigued professional. 'But if you must know, it was a Moorish physician by the name of Hatim al-Qurtubi.'

'Al-Qurtubi!'

Venerio's expression was one of such exaggerated amazement it took Galen aback.

'You've heard of him?'

'We met in Constantinople when we were both students. He's an arrogant bastard, but if he did all he could, then, much as it pains me to admit, he was probably right. What did he do, by the way?'

Galen had no wish to explain his treatment, for it would have to include what had happened to him.

'It was a surgery.'

'What kind—'

'Later, Venerio,' Fra' Martinus said. 'I grow tired. You can interrogate Brother Galen some other time.'

'Of course,' Venerio said, bowing deeply. 'I shall leave you to talk and return this evening.'

The abbot waved him away and Venerio gave Galen a nod of farewell that seemed to imply that he would search him out.

'So, you're the saint,' Fra' Martinus said.

Galen dismissed Venerio as a concern for later and hurried to kneel beside the bed.

'You surprise me,' Martinus said. 'You don't look like the usual run of people who come to Rome claiming to be a saint. Although the aesthetes starve themselves to look pale and virtuous, you are something else.'

'I don't know if I am a saint.'

Galen hadn't intended to whisper, but his voice failed him under the hard stare of this man.

'What do you mean, you don't know?'

'I don't understand what is happening to me. I'm just a scribe. I don't understand why miracles have happened around me, for I have done nothing to cause them.'

'But you can't be so ungrateful for this gift, can you? I mean, you came to Rome. You want to see the pope.'

'Bishop Sigburt wrote to the pope about me. I came at his command.'

'So there have been other miracles?'

'I think so,' Galen said, worried to be asked this when he knew Carbo and Alcuin had already told the abbot everything. The man was clearly testing him.

'You don't know?'

'I am not certain.'

'Why not?'

'Because I don't feel anything. Surely when a miracle happens, I should feel something?' Galen asked and wished he didn't sound desperate, but this was one of the questions that bothered him the most.

'How would I know? I've never seen a miracle. I've seen plenty of things that were claimed as miracles. I've read of even more instances of the fantastical, but I have always found some other sensible explanation.'

It surprised Galen to find himself in agreement with the abbot.

'People say it was a miracle we didn't drown when we were shipwrecked. But surely it would be more miraculous if we'd made it to Rome with no difficulties at all?'

Fra' Martinus gave a bark of laughter and said, 'Nobody would call a journey without incident miraculous.'

'But surely that would more clearly indicate the hand of God protecting us than a journey where we continually cheat death?'

'Ah,' Fra' Martinus said, 'but people wouldn't notice such a thing. They'd take that for granted. It's only when disaster narrowly misses them that they bless themselves, thank God, and tell all they meet of the wonders they've experienced.'

The way he spoke, and his tone of voice, struck Galen as odd. Then he realised why and failed to suppress the start that came with this. But perhaps it wasn't important, he thought, and started on a shrug that he quickly suppressed.

He was too late though - Fra' Marinus had noticed.

'You think you have discovered something about me?'

Galen started on a denial but he couldn't lie, even when it might be best to do so. He damned his all-too-transparent face then gave a quick nod.

'And what have you discovered?'

'You don't believe.'

Galen held his breath, his eyes fixed on the abbot, certain he'd said enough to have himself banished.

'What?!' Fra' Martinus said and started forward. That proved too much for him and he collapsed into his pillows again. 'How dare you say that about an abbot of a holy order?'

'Forgive me, I meant no offence,' Galen said, which was the absolute truth.

'That is not a retraction,' the abbot said, back to glaring at Galen. 'What makes you think I am a non-believer when we have barely exchanged a dozen words?'

'It's not your words, it's your attitude.'

'Because I doubt you are a saint? Are you offended?'

'I doubt I am a saint, too,' Galen said, fearing that he was sinking into a treacherous hole of his own making.

'So answer my question. What gave me away?'

Galen realised that was as close to an admission as the abbot could give.

'You ooze disbelief about saints and miracles.'

'I shall have to be more careful. In my youth I was a very devout young man, but age and time have shown me many things and the more I've seen, the less...' Fra' Martinus trailed off, waving his hand as if to dismiss the thought.

One that was too dangerous to voice. Galen nodded and his gaze slipped to the floor, waiting and wondering what would happen to him now and trying to ignore the pain in his knees from the hard wooden floor.

'What's this?' Fra' Martinus said. 'Are you not going to try to show me the error of my ways? Are you not going to tell me how I damn myself if I don't recant?'

'It is not for me to say such things.'

Galen had started to shake, whether from exhaustion or fear, he didn't know. It made him clasp his hands tighter together to keep them still.

'Can it be possible that you don't believe either?'

'No, I believe,' Galen said. 'With all my heart.'

'Then why don't you try to win me back to God?'

It was a fair question, and what the church would demand.

'It isn't my place to do such a thing, and I doubt I'd succeed even if I tried.'

'You wouldn't. But the least you could do was renounce me, have me beaten, stripped of my office and cast out.'

'To what purpose?'

The severity of the punishment the abbot suggested for himself astonished Galen, even when he knew most other monks would prescribe that same thing or worse.

'To what purpose? My boy, I am flabbergasted. I am leading my monks astray with my godless ways, am I not?'

'No.'

'You don't think so?'

'You wouldn't lead me astray. Why would you lead them astray? Each man walks the path chosen by them.'

'You are strangely pragmatic.'

'It is my nature. I wish I could lead you back to God's love, but I can't. Nobody can do that but you,' Galen said, as discomforted by the conversation as he was by the hard floor.

'People have their minds changed all the time. How else would they turn to cults and renounce the church? Surely that is due to a malign external power?'

'I think you would need to be inclined towards that already, or be driven by a need or desperation. I don't see that in you.'

'Quite the opposite really,' Fra' Martinus muttered. 'Now, get up and pull that chair closer. I can't have you squirming beside me. Or at least, I'd prefer to know why you are squirming.'

'Thank you,' Galen said and struggled to get up without putting too much pressure on the bed. Then he hobbled over to the chair and dragged it back, all the while trying to think about what the abbot had told him and what he should say.

The abbot watched him settle then said, 'Most men in my position would pray to God for healing and, if not that, then for salvation for their soul.'

Galen nodded. It was a terrifying thought that the man before him must accept that he was headed either for oblivion or hell and he seemed not to care about either.

'You could pray for me,' Fra' Martinus said, cocking his head to one side to get a better view of Galen's face.

'I could.'

'But would you do so if I didn't ask you to?'

Galen shrugged, aware that he was veering from the path of church-approved dogma and yet unable to stop himself from exploring these dangerous ideas with a man who wouldn't condemn him. Or, actually, couldn't condemn him. A man, moreover, with considerable learning.

'God is all powerful. If He wants you to know He exists, He will show you. I don't see how my prayers can change His mind.'

'It is church dogma that a saint can intercede. Some people are more beloved by God than others.'

'I don't think so. We are all equal in His eyes,' Galen said, digging up yet more bucketfuls of trouble from his unorthodox theological hole.

'You don't think you are loved by Him?' Fra' Martinus said. 'I must say, your arguments are more interesting than anything I've heard in a long time.'

'I use the same reasoning as with the shipwreck. If God loved me... loved me more than He loves others, my life would have been very different.'

'You feel you have suffered?'

'I have.'

'Huh, until I lay on this bed and felt my life slipping away, I lived a very comfortable life. My family is influential, my schooling was superior and I became an abbot at a young age. My monastery has always run smoothly and I have been able to avoid the politics which swirl around this city and have sucked many men in to destroy them.

'Yet you, who claim to have suffered, and judging by your frailty, this could well be true, you believe in God. Perhaps it requires a trial, a test of faith, to make a man really believe.'

'Then only men who have suffered would believe and that isn't the case.'

'True. You argue well. Are you sure you are only a scribe?'

Galen gave a quick nod and prayed they were moving to safer conversational territory.

'I have read as many books as I can lay my hands on. It has given me some knowledge.'

'So it would appear. Now, I will make you a deal. I will try to get you in to see the pope if you keep my secret in your breast and never reveal it to anyone.'

'You don't need the bargain. I wouldn't mention it anyway.'

'Why not?'

'It is no business of mine.'

'Some might say it was your duty to have my baleful influence removed from the monastery.'

'Perhaps.'

Galen's gaze sank once more to the floor and he trembled as he waited. He'd been frightened all the way through the interview and yet he'd foolishly said outrageous things he should have kept to himself.

'Can it be that while you believe in God,' Fra' Martinus said, 'you don't entirely subscribe to the laws laid down by the church?'

'I obey the requirements of my church and my order.'

'But you don't believe in them,' Fra' Martinus murmured, 'and when you don't see it as necessary, you ignore them.'

'There is no monastic rule which states that a godless man should be removed from office.'

'There is nothing on that very narrow topic, but there is plenty in the Bible to make you decide to unmask me. Corinthians makes it very clear: "do not be unequally yoked with unbelievers" and "bad company ruins good morals".'

'Are you bad company? Most of what the Bible says about non-believers is linked to acts of depravity,' Galen said. 'I don't know you, so I have no way of judging, but your abbey seems no different to any other I have visited.'

'That is not to say you found it to be good,' Fra' Martinus said. 'And what about this from Chronicles: "And they entered into a covenant to seek the Lord, the God of their fathers, with all their heart and with all their soul, but that whoever would not seek the Lord, the God of Israel, should be put to death, whether young or old, man or woman".'

'You have been doing your research. Why?' Galen said, as nausea welled up in his throat to be put so much to the test. His inclination was to leave well enough alone, but he wasn't sure if that was because of his yielding nature or his belief that God was more benevolent than the church. That said, the church overlooked some quite outrageous behaviour amongst its adherents too, especially those at the higher ranks.

'Why have I done my research?' Fra' Martinus said. 'Because I, too, have wondered about my morals, and my current position, and whether I should continue in it.'

'But why do you press me on this?' Galen asked, desperate to move on so that he could leave. He was playing with fire here. They both were. 'Do you want to be exposed?'

'Not at all. You're right, I shouldn't push you. And now I am tired. But, if I am strong enough, I'd like to return to this conversation.'

Galen shuddered but nodded, cursing himself for having said so much already. And yet, a part of him wondered whether it might not be interesting to delve some more into this murky water. Then he shook himself, to stop being so foolish.

'You dislike me,' Fra' Martinus said, misunderstanding Galen's shudder.

'I don't know you and I... I am not very good with people I don't know.'

'I was told you are shy.'

Galen nodded and his eyes flicked briefly up to the abbot's face.

'Still, I demand it as my payment. You want to see the pope and I can arrange that, although it will take time.'

'It will?' Galen said and put his hands on the arms of the chair in an unconscious gesture, as if he was about to rise, because he wanted to escape from this probing man.

'The pope is a busy and, it has to be said, restless man. He isn't easy to pin down. Although I fear he may disappoint you. He is young and probably no cleverer than you.' Galen gave a slight shrug and the abbot said, 'You'd best learn to school your face to give away less. I gather you don't expect much from the pope.'

'Alcuin had to continue on to Rome after Bishop Sigburt died because he promised he would. He also thought I might get some definitive answers from the pope. He knows all this talk of being a saint weighs on me.'

'But you had no such expectations and yet, still you came.'

'Alcuin thought it best.'

'And he leads you, does he?'

'He would always wonder what might have been if we didn't come.'

'It is a strange reason, young man, especially for one who clearly finds travel difficult.'

'Perhaps… deep in my heart, I still hope I will get answers too. I will never get the answers in Enga-lond.'

CHAPTER 4

Alcuin took one look at Galen's taut and tired face as he stepped out of the abbot's room and said, 'We'd best get you back to bed.' Galen stopped and gave him a surprised look which took Alcuin aback, for Galen seldom resisted him. 'You've had a hard couple of days, what with our long journey and the cult. You may be much improved from Hatim's surgery, but you still look worn down.'

'He's right,' Carbo rumbled. 'You're pale and shaky. It can't be good for you.'

'Please,' Alcuin said, noting the thoughts that flicked across Galen's face, which held a trace of unaccustomed irritation. 'You know it will do you good and Carbo and I will keep watch so you'll be safe.'

'What good friends you both are. I don't deserve this attention and care,' Galen said.

'Nonsense,' Carbo said. 'We'd do this for anyone who was as worn down as you.'

Galen grimaced his acknowledgement and allowed himself to be led back to the pilgrims' sleeping quarters and to his bed. This relieved Alcuin because Galen had emerged from his meeting far more rattled than expected. What had the fra' said to cause such disquiet?

It took a while for Galen to fall into a restless sleep, but when he did, Alcuin said, 'Brother Carbo, would you mind watching over Galen for a while?'

'Of course, that is why I am here. But where will you be?'

'I'll take this opportunity to settle us in. I had hoped we'd be able to see the pope within a matter of days of arriving in Rome. Now it's clear it will take longer. So I'm thinking we might join this abbey for the duration of our stay rather than remaining with the pilgrims.'

'Good idea,' Carbo said. 'I'd feel more comfortable if I were doing something useful.'

'You already are,' Alcuin said, giving the man a reassuring pat on his shoulder. 'But I know what you mean. My soul craves the familiarity of an abbey and a return to the work I should be doing.'

'That's a fact,' Carbo said on a deep sigh.

'I'll be quick. If Galen wakes before I return, you can reassure him of that.'

'I doubt he will wake,' Carbo said as he sat on the bed opposite Galen and gazed at him with the expression of a loyal dog who would not move an inch until his master was up again. 'He looked so tired I wasn't even sure of the wisdom of seeing the fra'. Not to mention that stoop when he walks.'

Alcuin had noticed the stoop had become more pronounced. It was an indication of how unwell Galen felt. He should have been pleased that Carbo noticed and wanted to do something about it too, but his jealousy couldn't allow it.

He chided himself for his pettishness as he said, 'I trust you to keep him safe.'

Then he hurried away before he changed his mind. What he was about to do was for everyone's benefit, not just his own.

Alcuin stepped out of the pilgrims' dormitory into the narrow courtyard, across through the church and into the wide covered corridor that surrounded the open cloister, heading to the porter's office. From his travels and a long-ago, half-remembered talk, Alcuin knew that most monasteries and abbeys conformed to a similar pattern. It was modified to suit the geography of the place, but it was in the same pattern as Yarmwick, or a mirror image.

San Agato's layout was a mirror image but also more cramped. The cloister he'd seen was smaller, while the church was bigger. The abbey bell tower was unimaginably tall, and the rest of the buildings were larger and taller and tiled in terracotta like the Moorish buildings, not the thatch of home. It gave him an odd sense of both familiarity and strangeness. He wished he could draw it and capture the shapes and configurations, but that would have to wait.

'Excuse me, Brother,' Alcuin said, tapping on the doorframe of the already open door to the porter's lodge.

The porter was currently slumped over his desk, his hood pulled low on his face, his arms crossed and his hands tucked inside his sleeves. He appeared to be napping. Alcuin knocked again, more loudly this time.

'Brother Donato!'

The old man grunted and his head snapped up so fast his hood slipped right off his head.

'What do you want? Bothering me at my work.'

'I do apologise, but I was hoping to speak to your prior.'

'And why would you need to do that? Isn't it enough that you've already spoken to our abbot? You think you're oh-so-important, don't you?'

Alcuin wanted to tell the porter that he was rude, but he held back. Old men didn't like the order of their days being disrupted.

'We just want to make ourselves useful,' Alcuin said as politely as he could. 'We will do whatever tasks are allocated to us.'

'Mmm,' the porter grunted, still glaring at Alcuin. 'What do you usually do?'

'I'm an illuminator and Galen is a scribe.'

'Then there's no need to bother the prior. He has enough work doing the job of the abbot on top of his own. I'll take you to see the armarius, Brother Iacopo.'

'Thank you.'

Alcuin wasn't sure about skipping the step of introducing himself to the prior, but if that was the way the porter wanted to do things he wouldn't object.

'Follow me,' Brother Donato said.

He hitched up his belt, then picked up a large ring filled with keys. He locked the door behind him and headed towards the church, right through it and into the part of the abbey that only monks could enter. They didn't mix with visitors or laymen, who also had their own dormitories, refectory and latrines. This allowed the monks to focus on the spiritual without the distractions of the mundane world.

Sometimes Alcuin regretted this rule, for it limited his view and starved him of images for his illustrations. Today, he felt a thrill of familiarity as if he were returning home.

'That's the refectory,' Brother Donato said, waving his ring of clanking keys at the building opposite. 'On the right are the kitchens, cellar and bakehouse.'

Alcuin hurried along, keeping a pace behind the man. He could have guessed about the kitchens because of the warm smell of baking bread and stewing vegetables.

To his left, three sides of an octagonal building poked out and he asked, 'Is that the chapter house?'

He assumed so, and already knew that it merged with the building that housed the dormitories for all the monks on the upper floor, along with their abbot's chambers.

'If you join us, you'll see it every day,' Donato said, looking peeved that Alcuin had jumped ahead of his monologue as they crossed the cloister and stepped into the refectory. It was dark and cool as it was long past mealtime.

They wove their way past the rows of tables, far more than Yarmwick ever needed, and out into a smaller cloister. The drone of someone reading the psalms escaped an open window in the building at the far end. It was such a familiar cadence and topic that Alcuin knew instantly that a lesson was in progress and he'd found the home of the novices; that and the latrines, if the faint smell of human faeces was any guide.

'Bathhouse to the right. In the taller, narrow building behind are the latrines,' Brother Donato said.

Alcuin was impressed with the latrines in this abbey. Even though they were in the middle of a city, they had engineered channels of water that flowed below, washing everything away.

'Now through the calefactory and you're at the scriptorium,' Brother Donato said, stopping before a pair of tall but simple double doors. 'I'll leave you here; the gate must be attended at all times, after all.'

'Thank you once again,' Alcuin said, since it was best to stay on the good side of the porter, even if he seemed to be a grumpy old soul.

It would have been nice to have been introduced, but, since that wasn't to be, Alcuin tapped and, without waiting, let himself in.

The scriptorium was bigger than Alcuin had expected. It was well lit, with larger windows than anywhere else in the abbey, although the vaulted ceiling with its curving stone spines was so high as to be dark. A section of the scriptorium jutted out, like a side chapel, with windows on both sides. Judging by the size of the desks, the vast quantities of pots of paints, and the sheets of vellum pinned to the wall with colourful arrays of images, many variations on a similar theme much like in his pattern books, Alcuin guessed that was the space for the illuminators.

His arrival also meant that every monk raised their head and turned to examine the newcomer. Their serious, unsmiling faces were intimidating, even for one who enjoyed meeting new people.

'Ah, good day,' Alcuin murmured. His voice sounded obscenely loud in the silence. 'I was told to speak to the armarius... Brother Iacopo?'

Now every head turned to the far end of the room where an old man with a pronounced hooked nose, band of white hair and flying white eyebrows, sat looking half surprised and half outraged.

'Who are you?' the old man asked, standing up. 'And why are you unaccompanied?'

'Ah, Brother Donato said he had to return to the gate,' Alcuin said as he walked briskly down the avenue between two rows of desks and bowed low before the armarius. 'I am Brother Alcuin from the abbey of Yarmwick in Enga-lond.'

'Oh you are, are you? And why should I care?'

Alcuin had given some thought on how to approach this question, although he hadn't expected to be challenged quite so aggressively.

'My traveling companion and I are in Rome to see the pope.' Alcuin rode the sniggers and gasps this statement elicited from the monks. 'But Fra' Martinus told us that will take a while.' That silenced everyone. 'We would therefore like to make ourselves useful. As I am an illuminator and Galen is a scribe, I thought I should speak to you first.'

'You're an illuminator, are you?'

'Yes, Brother.'

'From Enga-lond?'

'That's correct.'

'What makes you think you'll be up to the standard I require in my scriptorium?' Brother Iacopo asked and crossed his arms.

'I have made no such assumption. But in our homeland both Brother Galen and I are considered to be two of the best.'

'That's a bold claim,' one of the monks muttered.

Alcuin resisted looking behind him to find the speaker.

'We were called upon to produce a Book of Hours for our king.'

'That's as may be,' Brother Iacopo said, 'but here you will have to prove yourself. Brother Feo is our oldest illustrator. He specialised as a rubricator. Draw something for him. If you pass his test, I'll let you join my scriptorium.'

'Thank you for the opportunity.'

Alcuin felt like he had reverted to childhood to have his experience so dismissed. All the same, he walked over to a man who looked to be in his mid-thirties or early forties, with dark brown hair lightly streaked with grey and watery hazel eyes.

'I'll get the materials you need,' he said, giving Alcuin a nod. 'You may sit at my desk. Don't do anything too fancy, I'll get an idea of your style with whatever you produce.'

Alcuin wondered whether that was true. Since he was worried by how long this would take, and leaving Galen alone with Carbo, he spent only a few moments considering what to draw. He decided on two images that he'd doodled so many times he could probably draw them in his sleep. The first was a circle with three deer, their legs and antlers intertwined. The second was a picture of a monk fending off a snail with his quill; that one usually got a smile, and he needed something to win over the monks. He wondered whether Romans were inherently unhelpful, or if there was something about his approach that was putting their backs up. Either way, they were a brusque lot.

'Done,' he said, looking around for Brother Feo.

He was in the middle of dabbing his watering eyes with a handkerchief, which he shoved into his pocket before he bent over Alcuin's artwork, coming so close to the parchment he bumped his nose.

'Very nice,' he murmured. 'Very neat, and quick too.'

Brother Iacopo strolled over and the rest of the scriptorium took that as tacit permission to follow him so that Alcuin was surrounded by black-clad monks. The armarius also spent some time looking the image over.

'It is a very different style from what we do in Rome, but none can deny your skill. You may join the scriptorium.'

'Thank you,' Alcuin said and reached for the vellum, but it was snatched from the armarius's hands by a particularly swarthy and hairy monk, and the rest then tried to wrest it away from him.

Alcuin decided to let it go. It had served its purpose and gained his entry. Brother Iacopo's comments about the Roman style had also intrigued him. He hadn't considered that possibility and was filled with excitement that he might learn a great deal during his stay in Rome.

When Alcuin got back to the dormitory, Galen was still asleep and Carbo was in the same faithful guard position Alcuin had left him in hours ago.

'Everything alright?' Alcuin asked as he put down another steaming mug of herbal tea.

Carbo nodded, then glanced towards the other end of the dormitory at a pair of pilgrims in a mirror image of them, one man in the bed, the other seated beside, watching him. Carbo tilted his head and Alcuin followed him to the door that led to the cloister.

'There's something funny about those two,' he muttered in an undertone, keeping an eye on the men over Alcuin's shoulder.

'Funny in what way?'

Alcuin was never sure what to make of Carbo and his observations. Most times he seemed to be a simpleton. But he'd been a soldier in his past life and had a soldier's sense of danger that had already saved them once before.

'They arrived after the other pilgrims left, claiming the one in the bed is ill, but they're watching us. Not like strangers checking each other out. More like... stealing glances when they think I'm not looking.'

'Alright,' Alcuin said. It took some discipline not to turn and look - if they were being spied upon, it was best not to let on they'd noticed. 'But why?'

Carbo shrugged.

'Who knows what Bartolo may have said and whom he might have said it to after I dropped him off at his monastery.'

'But how would they have found us?'

'I'm pretty sure we mentioned where we were going to stay in Rome when we were still with that woman's cultists,' Carbo said, sinking his voice so far Alcuin had to lean closer to hear him.

'Well, we won't be in this dormitory much longer, so let's wait and see for now.'

'We're moving?'

Alcuin nodded.

'I'll tell you more when Galen wakes.'

'Alcuin?'

Galen's soft voice was barely heard over the sounds of the cooing pigeons but Alcuin felt like his ear had become attuned to his friend's voice and he hurried over.

'How are you feeling?'

'Better.'

'I'm glad to hear it,' Alcuin said, raising the mug of tea. 'I made the case that you are ill and managed to wrest this from the kitchen. It's a tea you know well.'

'Thank you, I am feeling much better,' Galen said, but it looked like it took an effort to sit up. 'What time is it?'

Alcuin waited till he was supported by the pillow Carbo had propped up against the wall before he handed the mug over and sat down beside Carbo.

'It's just past Vespers. At the risk of offending you, I think you should stay in bed for the rest of the day and see how you feel tomorrow before deciding whether you should get up.'

'You wouldn't offend me,' Galen said with a slight, shy smile.

'I just ride roughshod over you sometimes, I know. I will try not to do it in future.'

'Never roughshod, Alcuin. I am all too aware of how much you look after me and I am more grateful than I could ever tell you.'

'Nonsense. Besides, you have repaid me a hundredfold and more. Which, as I can see you squirming, I won't go on about.'

'Have you managed to do anything today or have you been tied to me all the time?'

'Carbo watched over you, and I met with the abbey's armarius who runs a very impressive scriptorium. I doubt there is anything in Enga-lond to equal it. He tells me theirs isn't even the best scriptorium in the city, although I gather it is amongst the best.'

'Alcuin… are you thinking of staying here?' Galen asked, and he looked horrified.

'Not at all, but winter is around the corner and the porter told me that the path back to Lundenburh goes over the Alps, which are even higher and more impressive than the Pyrenees, if you can believe that. It's cold to pass them even in summer and everyone is of the opinion that it's impossible to get through in winter.'

'So we're stuck here?'

'Only for the winter. We can head off in the spring. By which time we will hopefully have seen the pope.'

'This is going to take far longer than I'd hoped.'

'I'm afraid so, but in the meantime we can do something productive, can't we? The armarius said we can work in his scriptorium, which will be a good way to pay for our room and board. It will also give you a chance to look over some of the monastery's books. You'd like that, wouldn't you? We can also move in with the other monks. If you're like me, you'll prefer that to being in this common room with the pilgrims.'

'I would prefer to be with other monks, it's true. And you're sure you don't want to stay here permanently?'

'I have no intention of settling in Rome. I can't live so far from home. But while we wait, we may as well make the most of our stay. I've been itching to do some proper illustrations. Aside from that, there's a lot to be discovered in the abbey and in Rome; new books for you and new art techniques for me.'

Galen looked up and said, 'New art techniques? Is there something you can learn here?'

'The abbey is filled with inspiration. It's more sombre than the Moorish palace, but as different to home. Here it is much darker. Darker stones and darker wood, smaller windows too. But their church has a chapel of rare beauty.'

'Does it?'

'Oh Galen, the entire area around the altar is filled with a mosaic of John the Baptist surrounded by small gold tiles which shimmer and flash in the candlelight. It took my breath away.'

'It sounds wonderful.'

'It swept me into raptures and you know I'm not easily moved. That made me wonder what else we can see in Rome and I asked the armarius for permission to go out and see some points of pilgrimage ourselves.'

'Did he allow that?' Galen asked, looking surprised but also pleased.

'We are visitors and so have more freedoms than the monks who have sworn their lives to this abbey. Besides, I don't want you to sneak off like you did in Lundenburh and get into trouble. We'll go out together and do some proper sightseeing. Carbo can come with us too.'

Alcuin was currently filled with the milk of human kindness and willing to have Carbo insert himself into their usual fellowship of two, and not only because there was a possibility they were being followed.

Chapter 5

'Alcuin, I'm getting up,' Galen said.

He'd been in a fitful half asleep, half awake state since the bells had rung for Prime. Despite feeling more tired than he would like, Galen was determined to make up his own mind, assert his authority and be up for Terce.

This intention had grown stronger after his meeting with Fra' Martinus when Alcuin had practically ordered him to bed. For the first time, Galen resented being told what to do and wondered whether he should resist. Then he'd chided himself. After all Alcuin had done for him, how could he be so petulant as to push his friend away?

'If you're sure,' Alcuin said.

'I am. I should know my own mind by now.'

'By now?'

'You know... at my age. I should have been making my own decisions for a long time, and I haven't. I behave as though I'm still a child and allow people to treat me that way too.'

'I wouldn't say that. It's just that you're quite small.'

'Scrawny.'

'You might still grow.'

'I doubt it,' Galen said as he pushed himself out of bed. 'So shall we go to Terce together?'

'I was planning on suggesting you rest for today and we join the monks tomorrow. But if you are ready now, there is no reason to delay.'

'I am ready,' Galen said and clenched his fists to prevent himself from backing out. He was pleased he'd stood his ground, but he was also shaking with the fear of facing strange monks. 'What will we do after Terce?'

'We'll join the brothers at their chapter meeting. After that, we can move our possessions into the monks' dormitory and present ourselves to the armarius.'

'They don't waste time in this monastery, do they?' Galen said, fighting the sensation that he was being swept along again without control, even though this was his own doing. 'Where's Carbo?'

'Helping in the kitchen. He's the kind who doesn't like to sit around.'

'And he's good at making himself useful,' Galen said, but he was surprised.

Carbo had been particularly watchful, so much so that even Galen in his befuddled state had noticed. He'd also continually checked on a pair of pilgrims on the other side of the dormitory. Galen had been too tired to ask why, but had noted that Alcuin also checked on them when he was guarding Galen. Ah, and that was it, he'd felt guarded instead of merely having Alcuin's protective presence. He wondered why, but trusted that Alcuin would eventually tell him.

In the meantime, Galen fell into step with the people flowing into the church. There were so many scurrying black-clad figures it reminded Galen of an ant hill. The thought brought a smile to his face, which was vanquished as a quiver of fear ran through him, tightening his stomach. So many people and he didn't know any of them. He wasn't sure whether it was the intoxicating fumes of the incense, the multitude of wonders, or not being rested enough, but he grew dizzy and had to grab on to Alcuin to prevent himself from toppling over.

'Are you alright?' Alcuin mouthed.

Galen nodded.

'I should have left you to sleep,' Alcuin said.

Galen shook his head to say that Alcuin bore no part in the blame. It was his own choice.

After Terce, Galen remained steadfast in his refusal to go back to bed and Alcuin sighed and said, 'Very well, we will continue the day as planned.'

So Galen, Alcuin and Carbo followed the monks as they filed into a squat octagonal building with stone seating much in the manner of a Roman amphitheatre. It had high windows that you would need a stepladder to reach and which provided meagre light. Nobody spoke but the space was filled with the noise of boots and the coughs of two hundred monks.

It was just as well silence was a rule, Galen thought, otherwise Fra' Martinus would struggle to make himself heard. It surprised Galen that the abbot was present at the meeting. Despite how ravaged and thin his illness had made him, he looked formidable sitting in the first row of seats facing the double doors, the most senior brothers around him.

They were the image of power and Galen glanced up to see whether Alcuin had noticed. Yes, his gaze was fixed on the tableau of abbey leaders. No doubt it would turn into an image in one of his works some day.

Fra' Martinus banged his walking stick on the floor to draw everyone's attention.

'Welcome, brothers,' he said in a soft voice that nevertheless carried around the room. 'I pray you will forgive my extended absence from our meetings. I'm afraid my health does not improve and I urge my senior brothers to continue considering my replacement.'

Fra' Martinus stood up and, accompanied by two sturdy monks, walked to the centre of the chapter house and was assisted first to get down onto his knees and then down some more until he was lying face down on the floor.

'I pray forgiveness from God and my fellow brothers in Christ for having absented myself from our meetings and from the Divine Offices.'

It was a formality. Something any monk returning after a period of illness had to do. It was something Galen had done on many occasions at home.

It made him shudder to see the abbot doing it, knowing what he knew of him. All the same, at least his behaviour was exemplary. Once he was done, the two monks helped Fra' Martinus back to his feet and supported him to his seat.

Once he'd recovered his breath, he waved his hand in Galen and his friends' direction and said, 'Aside from my return, I will introduce you to three visiting brothers. Brothers Galen and Alcuin have come all the way from Enga-lond. They were part of a mission with Bishop Sigburt of Crowland, who sadly died at the hands of the Moors.'

This caused a ripple of surprised murmurs and Fra' Martinus raised his hand for silence.

'You will have an opportunity to ask them more about this during their stay. Brother Galen is a highly regarded scribe, and Brother Alcuin is renowned in his homeland as an artist. The big brother currently accompanying them is Brother Carbo, from the Monastery of St Peter in the Kingdom of Navarre. He has been Brothers Galen and Alcuin's guide and protector to Rome. I trust you will make our visitors welcome for the duration of their stay.'

Galen shrank as every face turned towards them. It was hard in the half light to read the expressions of these men. He hoped it was just within their culture to be an unsmiling lot, for they didn't look pleased or particularly welcoming. Then again, they didn't look at him as though he was an irredeemable sinner, which was an improvement on Yarmwick. Maybe this was his opportunity for a fresh start, although it felt too far from home.

'My abbot,' Brother Fransisco the terrier said, raising his hand, 'will we have to accommodate the visiting brothers for long?'

'As to that, I cannot say.'

'The thing is, our budget is tight and so is our space. To take in three extra men at this time...' he faded away, looking about the chapter house as if in search of allies.

'I have to agree,' said a very good-looking, athletic, middle-aged man who was sitting to the left of Fra' Martinus. 'We are already living on top of one another, and to arrange additional food and clothing at the start of winter, without prior warning, is a bit—'

Fra' Martinus held up his hand and said, 'Really chamberlain, you and our dear terrier are always the first to complain.'

'Our cellarer must surely have something to say on the matter too,' the chamberlain said.

'No doubt he has, and I'm sure he, too, will have a good reason why we can't take in these three. But I have even better reasons for taking them in. Mainly because the pope called for them. So, unless you want to feature as the men who threw out three monks summoned by our pontiff, you will accept our latest additions and make them welcome.'

'Very well, my abbot,' the chamberlain said, and the cellarer and terrier nodded grudgingly.

'Now on to other business,' Fra' Martinus said.

Galen was struck by how unwilling these Romans were to welcome guests. It was so different to the hospitality they could have expected at Yarmwick. He also noted how little the abbot had said about him or their mission. He'd kept it to the bare minimum and Galen was thankful for that. The last thing he wanted was rumours about miracles swirling about the monastery.

By the time they reached the scriptorium, Galen was in more pain than he cared to mention, although he was determined to go on. He couldn't understand why he felt so bad now after a full day and night in bed when he'd been able to spend a few days on the road without stopping to recuperate. Truly, there was no understanding his affliction.

'Are you ready?' Alcuin said as he stopped at the door.

'I would feel less nervous if our chapter house welcome had been warmer.'

'Aye, I'm afraid they aren't the friendliest of people. But in here we have nothing to be ashamed of. In fact, they are lucky to have the two of us.'

Alcuin's confidence always acted as a balm for Galen's nerves.

'They will be amazed by your artistic ability.'

'And with your neat handwriting,' Alcuin said.

Galen just smiled and nodded for Alcuin to open the door. He was grateful that Alcuin rated him so highly, but honestly, few people cared about perfect script.

The scriptorium was filled with chatting monks preparing for a day of work who fell silent as Galen and Alcuin entered. Galen drew back, using Alcuin's broad shoulders as cover from the curious gazes. Then he clenched his fists and stepped forward, trying to make eye contact. The men of Rome were swarthier than Anglo-Saxons and these monks, with their olive skin, dark hair and some sporting black beards, were an intimidating lot.

'This is Brother Iacopo, the armarius,' Alcuin said, leading Galen to the front of the room, nodding to the other monks as he passed them. 'We are ready to take on any task you wish to assign us, Brother.'

Galen shrank at Brother Iacopo's examination, aware of how plain, pale and insignificant he looked.

'So, you are a scribe?'

'Yes, Brother,' Galen said as he bobbed a bow and shot a quick look at the armarius.

'As you can see, I have no shortage of scribes,' Iacopo said as his hand swept across the room to encompass the five rows of desks, each seating six men. 'I can always find something for an illuminator to do, but not a scribe. So what use do I have for you, one who comes from such a far off, barbarian land?'

'It isn't a barbarian land,' Alcuin said. 'Our monasteries have produced some of the finest intellectuals and most learned manuscripts in the world.'

'That may be, but it doesn't answer my question. What am I to do with Brother Galen?'

The question surprised Galen because Alcuin had implied that everything was already agreed. Now he took a proper look at his surroundings while he considered how best to reply to the armarius's question. Aside from the rows of scribes, there were two more obvious sections: one of miniators producing the ornate capitals, while the other was the space nearest the windows where the illuminators were working. He had an immediate solution, but he wasn't sure how it would be taken, especially from one so young.

'I could... well, I could translate some texts for you... if that would be helpful. I don't want to be a burden to this monastery.'

'Translations? From which languages may I ask?' Iacopo said with a sardonic smile.

Alcuin looked like he wanted to give the man a sharp set down, but he stopped himself when he realised Galen was watching and waiting to see what he would do, hoping he wouldn't say anything. Alcuin must have realised this and waved his hand as if to say: very well, if you want to do things for yourself, I won't get in the way.

Galen turned back to Brother Iacopo and said, 'I realise I don't have much, but I have been told my Latin is good. I could correct some of the Latin that has been turned into the vernacular over the years and,' Galen said as he took a deep breath, 'and I have lately learned Moorish. I know that probably isn't useful, but—'

'Moorish?'

'Yes,' Galen said, trying to work out why the man looked so surprised. 'I have a treatise on their numbering system and their mathematics, which is very interesting. I'd be glad of the opportunity to work on it and perhaps translate it. That will also give me a chance to practise the language and consolidate it in my mind.'

Alcuin grinned broadly at Galen who felt a glow of confidence, for it seemed he'd gone up in the armarius's estimation. The man looked impressed that he could do anything in Moorish, let alone attempt a full-blown translation.

'May I see this text of which you speak?' Iacopo said faintly.

'Oh yes, certainly,' Galen said. 'I can fetch it for you now.'

'Does this mean you'll have him as a translator?'

Alcuin turned to follow Galen, but he didn't need him and waved that Alcuin should stay. It wasn't very much of a distance between the scriptorium and the dormitory.

'As to that, I can't say yet,' Iacopo said. 'I will have to try Brother Galen out first.'

Galen nodded and left at what he hoped looked like eager speed while trying not to aggravate his injury, thankful that everyone was already at work and he was unlikely to run into anyone else. At least not any monks. The lay brothers who cleaned didn't even pause in their work as they shook out the bedding and carried it away to be aired in the sunny cloister.

This was also like home. The monks, especially anyone who worked in the scriptorium, rarely interacted with the lay people. The monks who worked side by side with these men in the kitchens and the pilgrims' dormitory probably knew each other well. But laymen weren't qualified to be scribes. Most of them couldn't even write. At Yarmwick, they only entered the scriptorium to clean once the monks had gone to prayer or to have their meals.

Galen's intention had been to only take the book on numbers that Hatim had given him. But on further consideration, he decided to take all his books. That way, he could demonstrate any of his skills, should he be asked.

By the time Galen got back, the monks were all hard at work, their heads bowed over their scripts, with only the scratch of pens and the occasional cough, sniffle and throat clearing to break the silence. For a panicked moment, Galen couldn't see Alcuin either. Then a wave from the illustrators' area drew his attention. Alcuin was settled at one of the large desks, paintbrush in hand, a sheet of vellum and a rainbow of paint pots in front of him. He hadn't looked this happy in months.

'Do you want my help?' he mouthed.

Galen shook his head. Then he gathered his courage and went to the front of the room where Brother Iacopo was sorting a pile of codices. Galen stopped at a respectful distance and waited. When he got no response, he took another step forward and cleared his throat.

'Ah, you're back,' Brother Iacopo said.

Galen held out the manuscript of numbers for the armarius's inspection. His relationship with Brother Ranig, the armarius at Yarmwick, was so bad that it made his hands tremble with associated dread. This older man flipped the book open, running a calloused finger from left to right along a line of text. The wrong way for Arabic, Galen noted.

'I see you have already begun on a translation,' Iacopo said, tapping the blocky line of text below the flowing Arabic letters.

'Oh, yes... we had some time during our journey.'

'And what language is this?'

'It's my mother tongue, Englisc.'

'That will be of no use to us. You will have to produce a version in Latin.'

'Of course,' Galen said and felt a surge of excitement that the armarius appeared to have already decided he was to be a translator.

The old man leaned closer to the page, examining Galen's Englisc text minutely. Because of the size of the Arabic text, Galen had shrunk his usual writing himself, so he could understand why it was such a struggle to read.

'This is very neat,' Brother Iacopo said, and looked up to examine Galen as closely as he'd inspected the text. 'Brother Alcuin told me that the two of you produced a codex for your king. That is why I agreed to take him in as an illustrator. I see now why you were chosen as the scribe.'

Galen nodded since some sort of response was being waited for, but he had no idea what else to say.

'I have a new young scribe who has just entered the scriptorium. You could make yourself even more useful by mentoring him.'

The order astonished Galen. No one had ever been given into his care. Mainly because of his reputation and the fact that Yarmwick's armarius detested him.

'I... I will do my best,' Galen said, his words coming out at barely a whisper.

So this was what it was like to arrive at a place where he was judged purely on his achievements. It made his eyes sting and he bowed to hide it while he blinked to keep back the tears.

'I think you have already met him,' Brother Iacopo said and looked vaguely out into the scriptorium. 'Brother Piero?'

'Here, Brother Iacopo,' Piero said as he stood up and gave an awkward wave.

'You can guide Brother Galen on the functioning of this scriptorium, how to get vellum, pens, ink and so forth. In return, Brother Galen will teach you penmanship.'

Piero looked dubious but nodded and cleared the pile of discards that had filled the desk beside him. Galen didn't blame him for his reluctance. He was an unprepossessing stranger, after all, and a head shorter than his new charge. Still, he was filled with a glowing warmth to have been given two tasks, one wished for, one unexpected but not unwelcome.

'Here, Brother,' Piero said as he pounded the leather cushion on the seat, liberating a cloud of dust. 'It hasn't been used much since Brother Stefano retired. He was rather possessive of this seat that he occupied for nearly forty years, so nobody dared to use it after he left, despite it having the best light in the scriptorium.'

'Ah... I see,' Galen said, gazing up at the tall rectangular glass window that was twice the height of any window at Yarmwick. 'Is he... is he still at the abbey?'

'Brother Stefano? Why, yes,' Piero said, nodding, which set his dark curls below his tonsure bobbing. 'He is the oldest monk at San Agato and he is blessed with visions that grew stronger as his sight began to fail.'

'I see,' Galen murmured and hoped that the old scribe wouldn't take offence at his seat being taken.

It was probably a deliberate calculation on the part of the armarius to put a visitor to the abbey in the seat. The old scribe was less likely to complain. Especially if, as Galen hoped, they weren't going to remain for long at San Agato.

Chapter 6

Autumn turned to winter almost overnight and brought with it the return to the winter timetable in the abbey. In between settling in and adjusting to the new people and the increasing cold, it had dawned on Alcuin that Galen was trying to overcome his shyness and be less reliant upon others. It surprised Alcuin that he felt a twinge of regret at that. But at least he was also pleased for his friend. He supposed spending nearly the entire summer as a prisoner amongst strangers in Al-Andalus had helped Galen see he could cope on his own.

All the same, aside from Piero, Galen hadn't mustered up the courage to speak to any of the other men in the scriptorium and they'd already been at the abbey for a week. This, despite the fact that the armarius grew more pleased with Galen as each day passed. He didn't say it in words, but the satisfied smile whenever he looked at Galen's work showed that the young man's ability increasingly impressed Brother Iacopo.

Alcuin was happy for his friend and equally pleased with himself for engineering this opportunity for Galen to do the translating he'd always wanted to. Now all he had to do was get Galen interacting more.

Alcuin was already on good terms with all the monastery's illuminators and at least on speaking terms with everyone else in the scriptorium. Galen, on the other hand, shrank from the contact, hurried to his desk at the start of every day and kept his head down.

'Alright,' Brother Iacopo said, earlier than usual before Vespers one evening. 'Brother Luca is yawning so widely that if we don't stop now, we're liable to be swallowed whole.'

'Ah, I'm sorry Brother Iacopo,' Luca said, giving the armarius a broad grin while he scratched his stubbly, tonsured head. 'Today just feels like it has dragged.'

'It always drags for you,' Brother Feo said. 'I have never come across a lazier man in all my life.'

Alcuin had to agree. In the short time he and Galen had been in the scriptorium he had already gathered that the shapeless, pale and dough-like Luca was averse to any kind of work and prone to lie across his desk, resting his head on his arms. Such behaviour would never have been tolerated at Yarmwick, but Brother Iacopo was a far more relaxed armarius than Alcuin was used to. All he did was walk along the rows, inspecting his scribes' work, and flick Luca with a slim cane to wake him up and make him pick up his pen again.

'The light was fading anyway,' Luca said and waved a languid arm in the direction of the artists' annex. 'We scribes don't have as much light as you do.'

'Any excuse will do for you,' Brother Feo said.

Feo was the oldest of the miniators and his illuminated capitals impressed Alcuin. They had a subtlety and a maturity that he rarely saw in others' work. He had already learned a lot from just watching Feo at work.

'It is in his nature,' Brother Bosso said, rolling down the sleeves of his habit now that he'd stoppered his ink pots.

The hairiness of his arms fascinated Alcuin. All the men in the abbey were darker and hairier than he was used to, but Brother Bosso was on another level. His hair was as thick and wiry as that of a terrier, and his demeanour was similar. He was always digging away at mysteries and had asked Alcuin more questions about his life and their journey than anybody else here.

Now he strolled into the empty space between the artists' desks and the scribes' that was their corridor out, but also the gathering place for conversation. He leaned against the wall, looking down at Galen who was still fully immersed in his translation work. Brother Piero looked torn between following the example of the other monks or remaining by his mentor's side.

Alcuin found it amusing, then shook that thought away. The youth was fortunate to have Galen inducting him into his new role. Galen was taking the role seriously too and spent quite some time working with Piero on his penmanship and the little things like managing his workspace, accurate copying and keeping his pens sharp.

'So,' Brother Luca said, twisting around in his seat to take in the gathered brothers, his motto being why stand when you can sit? 'Fra' Martinus said our visiting brothers wish to see the pope.'

Galen froze at his work, then looked up, meeting Alcuin's eyes.

'It's why we set off for Rome in the first place, although our arrival was supposed to be grander than it turned out to be,' Alcuin said.

'You were coming with your bishop,' Brother Bosso said.

'Indeed, as was revealed at the chapter house.'

Feo laughed. 'And now we want to know more. In fact, we've been very patient, waiting until today to ask, for what else is there for us to do but work, pray and gossip?'

Alcuin wasn't really surprised that everyone wanted to know more about them. No doubt whatever was mentioned in the scriptorium would rapidly become common knowledge throughout the abbey.

'We were very junior staff accompanying the bishop's mission. Unfortunately, we were the only ones to survive.'

'But why continue if your main reason for coming to Rome no longer existed?' Luca said with another exhausted yawn. 'So much effort!'

'The bishop's dying wish was that we come. But I have heard that the pope isn't even in Rome at the moment?'

Alcuin had ended the last comment as a question. Firstly, to change the direction of the monks' probing. Secondly, to find out as much as they could about the pope without causing anyone to wonder why he was so interested in the man.

'He'll be back soon, don't worry,' Feo said. 'He daren't stay away for very long.'

'Why is that?' Alcuin asked, struck by the nods of agreement from the surrounding men.

'The situation in Rome is always unstable. It's wisest he stays here to maintain order.'

'What happened?'

It was always best, Alcuin thought, to be fully up to date on the politics of a place. Especially in a city like Rome and especially with what he and Galen already knew.

'Ah, well,' Brother Feo said, rubbing his stubbly chin thoughtfully, 'where would one even start?'

'At the beginning,' Brother Iacopo said as he settled side-on in one of the scribes' chairs. 'When the emperor made Gregory the pope, it wasn't without controversy.'

'He is so young. When he became pope two years ago, he was only twenty-three. And he was a Frank, not even a Roman,' Feo said. 'It caused consternation.'

'The Consul of Rome brought it upon himself,' Luca said.

'Brought what?' Alcuin asked, but with some trepidation.

'The war,' Iacopo said. 'Crescentius the Younger was the head of the Crescenzi family. They're the most powerful family in Rome. Or at least they were. When Emperor Otto was still too young to take the throne, Crescentius declared himself Patricius Romanorum — the Consul of Rome. The highest ranked noble and its de facto leader.'

'All the same, Brother Iacopo,' Brother Bosso said, 'Crescentius asked the emperor to nominate a pope when Pope John died.'

'Maybe, but Crescentius didn't like that the emperor nominated his cousin,' Iacopo said with the exaggerated shrug Alcuin was growing familiar with, along with the flamboyant hand gestures the Romans used.

'So what happened?' Alcuin asked.

'How can you not know what happens within your own church?' Brother Feo asked.

'Because we were prisoners of the Moors. After that we were walking towards Rome along a trail where few people knew much about the goings on of your great city,' Alcuin said, watching Galen as he spoke. He was looking increasingly alarmed. 'But you speak as if everything was resolved. So what happened?'

'For that, you should probably ask Brother Piero,' Luca said. 'His family was involved.'

'But not me,' Piero said, waving both hands frantically. 'I'm the youngest and I hold no interest for my family.'

'The nobility of Rome,' Iacopo said, taking pity on his youngest scribe, 'decided to install their own pope. He took the name of John XVI.'

'That's simplifying it too much,' Feo said. 'Crescentius, had always given the previous pope problems, vying with him as the ruler of Rome. Which was why it came as a surprise when he let the emperor choose his own pope.'

'Or maybe he was just afraid of the emperor's power,' Luca said. 'After all, the emperor was threatening to have Crescentius banished.'

'And ironically, the new pope pleaded his case for him, and Crescentius got to stay.'

'Was that when he installed his own challenger pope?' Alcuin said. 'I'm impressed by his audacity.'

'His arrogance,' Bosso said, his gaze drifting over to Piero. 'We are all from noble houses, but none as exalted as the Crescenzi. He thought himself invulnerable and led a rebellion against the pope and all the installed Frankish dignitaries.'

'Such blatant rebellion is dangerous.'

'Very,' Iacopo said. 'Last year, the emperor returned to Rome and crushed the rebellion. He captured the anti-pope when he attempted to flee and laid siege to Castel Sant'Angelo, where Crescentius took refuge. While they waited for the siege to be broken, the anti-pope was publicly humiliated. I always thought that was counterproductive. It only made Crescentius hang on longer.'

'What did the emperor do to the anti-pope?'

'He was stripped and made to ride naked through the streets of Rome on the back of an ass. Then they cut off his ears and nose, plucked out his eyes and ripped out his tongue. They might have executed him after that, but Saint Nilus of Rossano interceded on his behalf and he was sent to a monastery in the Frankish empire. Then the siege to get Crescentius was broken. He was hauled out of Castel Sant'Angelo and executed, his body left to rot on a gibbet on Monte Mario.'

Alcuin glanced at Galen again, who was staring open-mouthed at the brothers, listening to the tale. He looked horrified, although not as much as Alcuin might have expected. Then again, rebels usually came to this kind of sticky end.

Alcuin was wondering whether it was safe to ask the monks' opinions of the current pope's personality when the bells rang, calling them to prayer. Everyone hurried out of the scriptorium, and Alcuin held out his hand to Galen in an offer of support.

'That was quite interesting, wasn't it?'

'It gives some insight into Pope Gregory,' Galen said. 'It seems when he was first instated, he wanted to be a benevolent pope.'

'Forgiving Crescentius, you mean?'

'Yes.' Since Galen was slow, they had fallen behind and were most likely out of earshot. 'But it is also clear he will only be forgiving up to a point.'

'He may be young, but he is a politician.'

'That is what I fear.'

Galen was trembling and Alcuin suspected not merely from his illness.

'Was the conversation difficult for you?'

'It wasn't so bad because nobody tried to draw me out and I knew you would intercede even if they did.'

'I would, but I got the impression you wanted to push yourself out a bit more.'

'So perceptive,' Galen said with his slight smile. 'I do. There's just so many of them and they talk so loudly.'

'They're more boisterous than our brothers back home, that's for certain. Shouting doesn't seem to be frowned upon as much as it is in Enga-lond either.'

'And their Latin is different, too. Sometimes I can hardly understand it.'

'I know. Their accent is atrocious.'

'Different to Carbo's and the monks of his monastery.'

'Theirs was even harder to understand. It's true.'

'It's interesting,' Galen said. 'And it isn't only the accent. They use some Latin words that aren't familiar to me. I've started making a list of all the different words.'

'Where? In your notebook? There surely can't be much space left in it.'

'It is getting a little cramped, but I can still find space.'

'I'm glad you're finding something to keep you busy and amused,' Alcuin said, then paused and made doubly sure they couldn't be overheard. 'I know you'll always watch what you say, but I feel around here it is doubly important to do so.'

'Is there something particularly worrying you?' Galen asked, looking instantly more alarmed.

This was why Alcuin hadn't mentioned the pilgrims that he'd become certain had been spying upon them. Galen was anxious enough as it was.

'Maybe just tense because of the highly charged political nature of Rome, especially knowing what we do,' Alcuin said, keeping it vague just in case. The last thing he'd do was mention Marozia's name.

CHapTer 7

Galen sat in the refectory beside Alcuin, halfway down the end table. It wasn't a spot of high rank - the most important people in the abbey sat at the main table that ran perpendicular to the tables occupied by the rest of the monks - but it made both their positions higher than Galen had been given before. He was older now. That accounted for it. He'd gained the seniority of age.

Thankfully, the large crowd of men warmed the room on what was a chilly, wet November day. Otherwise the cold would have robbed Galen of the pleasure he took from the serenity of this refectory with its whitewashed walls, terracotta floors and a large mural of the miracle of the loaves and the fishes behind the abbot's table.

It was Brother Luca's turn to read the lesson for the day, something he'd complained about vocally on their way to the refectory. Firstly, because he would have to stand while he read all the way through dinner. Secondly, because he could only eat once everyone else was finished.

'At least you will get extras, for having been the reader,' Brother Bosso had said as they'd made their way from the scriptorium to the refectory, although it was a perfunctory comment.

Brother Luca complained about anything that involved standing and everyone ignored him or teased him about it. Now he was reading an excerpt from the lives of the Roman Saints, Basilissa and Anastasia. It was interesting for Galen because he'd never heard of them before.

The reading was about lessons to be learned from their lives, of course, rather than their own thoughts, and had been written a few hundred years after their deaths. Which was all salient information for Galen as he tried to work out how a saint should act and feel.

Apparently, the two women had been some of the first converts to Christianity and had buried both the bodies of Saint Peter and Saint Paul after they were martyred. They'd been women of high rank who sounded like they'd been very active and helped to bury many more Christians with the proper rites during a time when it was illegal to be a Christian.

Galen wondered what the two women made of being saints. They were the kind he admired most, the ones who made a difference to other people's lives. Or perhaps that was just how they were portrayed now: women who weren't afraid to practise their faith and who were martyred for it.

Who knew how they had really felt at the time? How afraid had they been, sneaking about at night ensuring the burial of fellow Christians? Surely they must have shaken with terror to be doing something that would lead to gruesome torture and execution.

Alcuin nudged Galen and slid the plate of pigeon eggs closer to him. It was their supplementary food today and Alcuin, as ever, was scrupulous about sharing their portion exactly in half. Two of the little pure white eggs for him and two for Galen.

Galen tapped the point of the egg on the plate to crack the shell and started peeling. It was funny how he had a dual sense of familiarity and otherness in this place. It wasn't surprising, as every Benedictine order was run by the same rules. There were slight variations, but they were hardly worth mentioning. This abbey, for instance, ate more meat than the monks of Yarmwick. Their large pigeon loft provided a regular supply of both pigeon meat and eggs. They also used more olive oil than lard and never any butter. Galen was accustomed to this from his stay in Hatim's palace, but he noted that Alcuin still grimaced when he ate.

It was one difference between them. While Alcuin thrived on visual stimulation and could spend hours examining the intricate pattern on a series of tiles, it was almost as if his thirst for novelty ended there. For the rest, he seemed to crave the familiar. Whereas Galen, despite the pain he had to endure, liked the discovery of the new. He only wished he knew whether they would eventually be allowed to go back home.

The meal ended, as always, on a prayer, and the monks pulled their hoods back up and started heading back to their various tasks. At that moment, the young monk who had lately been accompanying the abbot hurried over, handed Galen a note and then made his way after Fra' Martinus who was disappearing into the cloister.

Alcuin waited until they, too, were in the cloister and watched as Galen unfolded the note. The contents were brief.

I would like a word. Come and see me in the lady chapel — on your own.

Galen handed the note to Alcuin, worrying about the comment to come alone. Did it mean the abbot wanted to continue pushing Galen over the question of faith? He hoped not.

He'd spent a lot of hours in prayerful contemplation, asking God what he should do. The answer always seemed to be the same. He had his path to walk and so did the abbot. It was the abbot's God-given right to make that decision, but he knew full well the church would disagree.

'Will you be alright?' Alcuin asked.

Galen smiled at him. Neither of them had any choice, but he was trying to show that he could be more independent.

'I'll be fine.'

Alcuin examined his face, probably reading all of Galen's fear and self-doubt.

'I'll see you in the scriptorium, then.'

Galen watched Alcuin catch up to the other scribes and illustrators who made a gap to allow him in, as if it were the most natural thing to do. But Galen knew that if he'd approached them, they wouldn't even realise he was there. He shrugged that melancholy thought away and told himself it was more because of his height than his lack of presence that people didn't notice him.

Then, keeping to the covered walkway that surrounded the cloister because it was raining heavily, he walked around to the side door that led into the church. It was darker than usual, another consequence of the rain, but Galen was familiar enough with the church now to head unerringly to the lady chapel.

The young monk was hovering at the entrance, obviously waiting for Galen, and looked relieved to spot him. Galen gave him what he hoped was a calm smile and, as the young man was indicating with both hands that he should enter the chapel, he did as ordered. It did not surprise him that, instead of following him in, the monk swung the wrought iron gate shut behind Galen. Obviously, the abbot intended to keep their meeting private.

So he walked the few steps to the front of the small chapel where the abbot was kneeling before a simple altar. A beautiful, lifelike sculpture of the Madonna and child, lit by a pair of fat candles, smiled serenely down at him from the large alcove behind the altar.

'Join me, Brother Galen,' Fra' Martinus said without raising his head from the praying position.

Perhaps he couldn't. He looked so skeletal that maybe he needed to keep his head propped up on his hands.

'Thank you,' Galen said, mindful of the fact that he was being awarded a great honour to spend time with the abbot, even if it took a great deal of effort to lower himself onto his knees.

At least he could use the same railing the abbot was using to aid his descent. He was still breathing heavily when he was finally down.

'I apologise for making you do something that takes so much effort,' the abbot said. 'If I'd known you would struggle, I'd have arranged another way to meet.'

'It's alright,' Galen said, speaking as softly as the abbot. To anyone listening from a distance, it would sound as if they were whispering their way through prayers. But a more troubling question was at the forefront of his mind. 'May I ask why it would be difficult to meet otherwise?'

'I am trying not to look like I'm singling you out. If you keep coming to my room, people might become suspicious. This way, others might think it a mere coincidence.'

'I see,' Galen said, although he wasn't entirely sure this would work as an excuse.

Then again, Alcuin wouldn't have to explain his absence from the scriptorium because Galen already had a special dispensation to absent himself from work whenever he needed to recover. People would therefore draw their own conclusions.

'Brother Ricardo will also keep his mouth shut, for I have ordered him to do so. And he will keep any others from approaching the chapel, so we may talk in peace.'

Fra' Martinus's words seemed to confirm Galen's fear that he wanted to discuss matters of faith. Galen didn't feel ready and blurted out, 'Why do you move from one junior assistant to another? First Brother Piero and now Brother Ricardo.'

'There is no great mystery to that. I like to get to know all the men under my authority. Any new monk who comes to the abbey will work directly for me for a few months before being assigned to their regular duties. If you and Brother Alcuin were to become full members of this abbey, I would have you do the same thing.'

'I see.'

It impressed Galen that the abbot was that thoughtful. He'd heard about other abbots who were so aloof they barely spoke to their monks. Others demanded excessive levels of respect, even insisting all their monks go down on their knees and bow their heads when the abbot passed by. Fra' Martinus, at least, didn't go to such lengths, although he took all the respect that was owed him.

'There is no need to fear our conversation,' the abbot said, accurately reading Galen's face. 'I have something of a request or perhaps a deal to discuss with you.'

Galen blinked at the man. What could he possibly do for the abbot? He might have suspected he'd be asked to perform a miracle if he was a believer, but that didn't seem to be the case.

'Anything within my power.'

'Be careful with promises like that,' Fra' Martinus said and turned back to staring up at the Madonna. 'Even though you come from a noble house in your lands, and must be used to some of the politics of power, it's on another level in Rome.'

'So I have been told,' Galen said and had to agree, even from the little he'd already seen of the place.

'Nothing comes for free here. People trade favours and goodwill the same way they trade money. To have influence, you must have something that others want.'

'I don't understand what that has to do with me.'

'You want to see the pope. To do that, I need something to bargain with.'

'But the pope summoned our bishop.'

'He is no longer with you. Now, I could call in one of the many favours owed to me by the cardinals of Rome and get you in, or I could tell a few well-placed people you are a saint. That might get you in.'

'No, I don't want to do that,' Galen said. 'Until I know for certain what is going on, I don't want to make any claims.'

'That is probably sensible. And in terms of what I just said, it's best not to trade on your reputation lest you become somebody's pawn.'

Galen had already felt like Bishop Sigburt's pawn. He didn't want to fall into more powerful hands. Which led to a second concern.

'Is it... is it likely the pope might try to use me, too?'

'I'd say inevitable. If you can raise his prestige, he will see a use for you and will keep you by his side. If you challenge him, however... well, I don't suppose he'll have you executed, but he'd probably bury you in some obscure monastery.'

'My abbey of Yarmwick?' Galen asked hopefully.

The abbot gave a cynical laugh and turned to examine Galen's face.

'Such optimism,' he murmured. 'He is more likely to keep you somewhere he can easily lay his hands upon you when needed.'

'I see,' Galen said and couldn't suppress a shudder. 'Would any pope be like that?'

'You're wondering about the character of this pope, are you?'

Galen feared saying anything at all on this topic, so just shrugged.

'He could be on the papal throne for decades to come,' Fra' Martinus said. 'You can't wait around for his replacement who will also see you only as an object to be used to further his own political aims.'

'It was a mistake to come to Rome.'

'Perhaps. But in the meantime, you can do something that might give you some leverage of your own.'

'I can?'

'The woman, Marozia,' Fra' Martinus said and now he looked like he was staring not at the Madonna but into some distant future. 'She came from a powerful family. Some who were concubines and mothers to popes, but also who number powerful bureaucrats such as judges and even a grand duke. Although they lost much influence as their rivals tried to root them out of the Lateran Palace, they still have a great deal of influence, especially amongst the cardinals.'

Galen's mind was racing, trying to understand what Fra' Martinus might be about to suggest and any counters he could offer.

'I have maintained cordial relations with as many of the powerful men of Rome as I can. Amongst them is the patriarch of the Theophylacti. We correspond regularly, partly because he is, surprisingly, of the same mind as I am when it comes to religion, and also because we are of a similar age and, currently, state of health.'

Galen wanted to stop the abbot right there, for he was getting an uncomfortable feeling about where this conversation was heading. On top of that, he feared the abbot might betray them.

'In his latest missive,' the abbot continued, oblivious to Galen's concerns, 'he mentioned his anxiety over his granddaughter, who was last seen on the road to Rome. Apparently, he'd been looking forward to seeing her.'

'Ah,' Galen whispered.

'You could at least tell him what happened. It won't bring him joy, but he'll not wonder for the rest of his life about the ultimate fate of his beloved family member.'

It was a cruel way to put it, for Galen could relate to the agony of not knowing.

'Is that wise?' Galen asked, for he felt like it merely shifted his pawn status from one pair of hands to another.

'You might learn more about the pope from them and you will gain a powerful ally into the bargain.'

'By giving them this sorrowful news?'

'A debt is a debt and if there is one thing you can be guaranteed, a Roman will always repay a debt, even if it takes a lifetime before you call it in. That's not to mention your status as a probable saint. I will not mention that to them, and you shouldn't either, not unless you can help it.'

'So they already know about me?'

'I have not yet mentioned you. But if you are willing, I will send a carefully worded missive and arrange a meeting. It won't be here or anywhere considered their territory. All sides will work to minimise the risk.'

The abbot's words brought little comfort, but Galen said, 'I will meet them.'

CHAPTER 8

'Here,' Galen said, handing Brother Piero his battered and moth-eaten copy of Boethius.
· He'd been waiting patiently for this chance to speak to Piero before they all headed to None and then dinner.

'What is it?' the young man asked, looking up from his desk where he'd just finished the last line of a contract between a local baron and a merchant.

'Something a bit more interesting to work on,' Galen said. 'I remember all too well the early days of my life as a scribe. They give juniors the most boring stuff.'

'All I've worked on so far are contracts and letters.'

'It's important work and provides funds for the abbey, but it can be disheartening to only have that to work on, so I asked Brother Iacopo if I could give you a side project. He said you can work on it as long as you finish all your other copying allocated each day.'

Piero brightened up at the suggestion, which relieved Galen. He'd been worrying for the young man whenever he gave a profound sigh in the midst of his transcription. At least having a charge of his own had given Galen the courage to make his request to the armarius. Despite knowing Brother Iacopo was nothing like Brother Ranig in Yarmwick, he'd still shaken while talking to him and was surprised when the man had accepted his suggestion.

'This is a book called the Consolation of Philosophy, which was written by a very great scribe. His life's work was to translate as many of the works of the ancient Greeks as he could. The influence of the ancient heathen philosophers such as Plato and Aristotle runs through this work and makes it quite different from anything else you'll have come across before.'

'Am I really allowed to work on such a piece? Isn't it heretical?'

'Boethius was a Christian and worked hard to reconcile Christian theology with the works of the Greek philosophers. He is accepted within our canon.'

'Then I will gladly make a copy. Thank you, Brother Galen.'

Galen swelled with pride, happy to have cheered up his charge. Not everyone would welcome being given extra copying to do at the end of the day.

His joy turned to worry as Fra' Martinus's assistant arrived and gave a slight bow.

'Yes?' Galen said.

'Fra' Martinus wants you to know that he is granting you permission to leave the abbey this Sunday for your requested pilgrimage. He recommends you take Brothers Alcuin, Carbo and Piero with you.'

'Oh, thank you,' Galen said, turning red as he realised the entire scriptorium had turned to watch this exchange.

'The fra' said that you should visit the Church of Saint Cosmo and Saint Damiano on your way back from St Peter's, as both saints are associated with healing.'

'Oh yes, of course,' Galen said and wished this wasn't being broadcast and thus drawing everyone's attention.

This walk was more than just a pilgrimage. This was the prearranged signal that the fra' had organised the meeting with a representative of the Theophylacti. Innocuous as it probably sounded to everyone else, it felt dangerous to be talking so openly about it in front of everyone.

Alcuin, who had already been told everything, must have read his thoughts and smiled as he ambled over, the rest of the illustrators joining him.

'At last, we can take in some of the holy places of Rome. I'm really looking forward to it.'

He spoke loudly enough that everyone heard and turned from watching Galen to Alcuin.

'Rather you than me,' Luca said with a gusty sigh. 'My curse is that I should have been born a noble woman, then I could have stayed in bed all day.'

'No,' Galen said softly, then blanched as everyone turned to looking at him. 'I... I—' he stopped and looked frantically at Alcuin.

'My friend is trying to say that noble women work a lot harder than we assume.'

'Yes,' Galen murmured, flushing with embarrassment that he had had to be rescued. 'They run the house,' he managed to add before his shyness overcame him again.

'That's true,' Feo said. 'My mother was always the first one up in my home, and the last one to bed. I think that was what wore her out and sent her to an early grave.'

'Well then, not a noble woman,' Luca said. 'But there must surely be one path of life that involves a lot of sleep.'

'A shepherd?' one monk suggested.

'No, they have a job keeping their animals together and safe from dogs, wolves, bears and even lions in the mountains,' Brother Bosso said.

'You would know, you're from the countryside, aren't you?' Luca said.

'And very glad to be away from it. There are far too many wild beasts to be comfortable.'

'We came across a lion,' Alcuin said.

Everyone fell silent for a moment and looked at the two of them.

'In the mountains when we were escaping from the Moors,' Alcuin added for good measure.

'You and Brother Galen?' Feo said, emphasising the and.

'Oh yes.'

'When you were escaping from Moors? You haven't told us this before,' Luca said, looking far more interested in Galen and Alcuin than he had ever seemed before.

'You have never asked me and Galen about our journey to Rome.'

'There are so many people who journey to Rome. It would become boring if we heard all their tales.'

'Not ours,' Alcuin said.

'Alright,' Luca said with a big grin, 'tell us all about it.'

So Alcuin, watched by a horrified Galen, began on the tale of their journey, starting at Lundenburh, including the vikings, the chase, their capture by the Moors and their escape, but leaving out any word of miracles and illness.

'That is quite a tale,' Brother Feo said. 'And while I can believe you were capable of it, I find it hard, forgive me if I say this, to believe that Brother Galen could also have gone through the same. He is far too frail.'

'He's tougher than he looks,' Alcuin said.

'Alcuin helped me,' Galen muttered, turning deep red.

'Well, that is impressive,' Luca said, 'but not restful enough. I would hate to go on a pilgrimage. Think of all those days of walking. Think of the blisters. No, not for me, thank you. I will stay in Rome, and perhaps I'll grow frail too and be able to spend my days in bed.'

'It isn't very pleasant,' Galen said, his eyes glued to the floor.

'How would I know if I have never been allowed to try it?'

'Enough of this chatter,' Iacopo said as the bells started chiming, calling the monks to prayer. 'We will be late for None if we continue this discussion. A very unedifying one at that, Brother Luca. You should pray to God to make you more worthy of the role you have been given in life.'

Chapter 9

'That was easier than I expected,' Galen said as he looked back at the imposing armoured door of the monastery.

'Why would the porter stop us with our dispensation from the abbot?' Alcuin said and pulled his cloak more tightly about himself to protect from the wind that funnelled down the narrow street.

'He accepted that?'

'Why wouldn't he?'

It was in Galen's nature to expect his path to be barred. Alcuin's expectations were the exact opposite. So, while Galen's heart drummed with fear when they'd approached the porter, Alcuin had no doubts about being let out.

'You've always had a way of speaking that leaves people unable to question or deny your will.'

'My abiding flaw,' Alcuin said and flushed, which surprised Galen.

'It is a very authoritative manner.'

'Which I use on you?'

'Sometimes.'

'I'm sorry, Galen. It isn't a conscious thing.'

'I don't mind. Maybe one day I'll learn how to emulate it,' Galen said as he took Carbo's arm and, leaning on the man, set off at a slow pace out into Rome. His guts always ached, so, for an outing, he needed to pace himself and accept help.

'Where to, Brother Pietro?' Galen asked as the young man was hovering, apparently trying to decide whether or not he should speak.

'We need to head northwest. It isn't very far, but it might be slow going as we'll have to keep an eye out for trouble.'

'What kind of trouble?' Carbo asked, lifting the heavy staff he'd brought with him and giving it a waggle.

Piero didn't look reassured.

'Anything from drunken revellers to thieves and warring factions.'

'Warring factions?'

Piero pointed his finger at a half dozen tall, well-fortified towers that loomed over the rooftops.

'Those aren't for show. They are the towers of the local nobility. They're always feuding. Fights between the knights of the different families can flare up and sweep down a street before you're even aware of what's happening.'

'Savages,' Carbo said, looking up at the thick stone walls, imposing tower and solid wood and iron gate of one such mansion opposite them.

Galen felt like it should intimidate him but the thrill of actually being in Rome dulled his fear. He'd often wondered what Rome would be like as he'd worked through his Latin as a boy. He'd thought it had to be an unrivalled city, and it did impress him.

'This must be the biggest, most populated place we've ever been,' Galen said, not even trying to mask his awe and excitement.

Alcuin looked less thrilled.

'I think bigger even than Hatim's home. Not that we got to venture out onto their streets.'

The rumble of carts trundling over cobbles, the clip clop of pack animals, the shopkeepers shouting their wares from open-fronted establishments, the bark of dogs, the squeal of pigs, even the cooing of pigeons and the chatter of the crowds set up such a din that Alcuin had to raise his voice to be heard over it all.

Galen nodded and reached into his pocket for his handkerchief to cover his nose. It wasn't just the noise. The stink of thousands of people and their livestock was overwhelming, despite their superior sewer system.

'Plenty of inspiration for your images though,' Galen said, pointing up at the white wall of a shop covered in painted messages about the wonders of wine.

Even at this early hour business was brisk, argumentative and sometimes physical. Carbo had to guide Galen around one vendor who held up a tunic while the buyer disputed the value of the item. Galen could only guess that from their body language, for he couldn't understand what the men were saying.

The language here was even stranger than in the abbey. Galen had expected to hear a pure form of Latin in the city of its birth. But they'd either got their Latin wrong in Enga-lond, or the inhabitants of Rome had bastardised their tongue to a point where it was still readable, but when spoken as rapidly as the natives did, with an unfamiliar accent, completely unintelligible.

Galen was still mulling over this drift of language when they stepped out of the crush of houses and shops and he found himself at the entrance to a wide Roman bridge. In a rocky ravine below was a river.

'The Tiber,' Piero said.

'It's considerably reduced from the river we followed into the city,' Galen said, then looked across the bridge to an enormous circular tower. It looked short and squat, yet it was higher than any of the surrounding towers.

'That's the Castel Sant'Angelo where Crescentius took refuge. Along with my father.'

'Your father was part of the rebellion?' Galen asked, wondering why the young man would tell them such a thing. 'Is your home visible from here, Brother Piero?'

'Oh... yes,' Piero said, colouring as he swivelled around and looked downstream along the Tiber. 'You see that tall tower with the greenish-blue tiles around the upper windows and the marble sculptures at each corner?'

'I see it,' Galen said and noted that Alcuin was also giving it an impressed stare. 'It's one of the largest towers in the area.'

'It belongs to the Hateria, my family.'

'Your father must be a wealthy man indeed,' Alcuin said.

'My father died alongside Crescentius,' Piero said in a calm, emotionless way.

'I'm sorry,' Galen said and rested his hand on the young man's arm.

He shrugged as if to say that was the way of the world.

'My eldest brother is now the baron.'

'And you are the youngest?'

'I am the youngest child, and the eleventh son. So you can see that there was not much use keeping me around. Half my brothers died in the battle that claimed my father's life, and my eldest brother killed a couple more to ensure his ascension to patriarch of the family.'

'And you?'

'I was given a choice: be thrown out and seek my fortune, or be given to the church with the funds to sustain myself in my new life.'

'They forced you into it.'

It wasn't an unfamiliar story. Galen's own might have been similar, although he had always wanted to join a holy order.

'It suited my brother's politics and keeps the new pope at bay by showing his allegiance to the church. He also sent my three remaining unmarried sisters to a nunnery.'

'So that was how you came to be at San Agato.'

Piero nodded, then turned and examined Galen more closely with his deep brown eyes.

'What I have told you is the truth, Brother Galen, but you should beware of lies and rumours. Don't believe anything you see in Rome and don't trust anything you hear.'

'Galen is too trusting,' Alcuin said, but his smile took the sting out of his words. 'We will try our best to be careful.'

Brother Piero nodded, all the while giving Galen a worried look which was followed by an expressive shrug.

'We're nearly at St Peter's.'

'That would explain the increase in the number of pilgrims,' Carbo said as he pushed away a ragged man who came too close to Galen.

'This is the only bridge leading to the basilica,' Piero said, 'so we are bound to see far more pilgrims from here onwards.'

As one of the most holy sites in the world, St Peter's was a massive draw for pilgrims. Galen felt his own excitement growing to such an extent he barely noticed the pain that had increased in his guts as they'd been walking. Although he leaned on Carbo's arm even more heavily, it was now for courage as well as support.

'I have never seen so many pilgrims,' Alcuin said as they reached the base of the Castel Sant'Angelo and turned left along a dead straight lane.

'There are thousands,' Galen said as his eye followed along the lane to a wide square humming with people. Hundreds of black-robed monks and nuns were clustered amongst the pilgrims who represented every walk of life. There were the rich, some carried on litters with a bevy of servants keeping others away from their masters, and there were the sick, dying and destitute. Some looked so frail Galen feared they might never leave this place.

At the end of the square was a portico the width and height of which Galen could hardly comprehend. It was so big that those in the queue of jostling, over-eager people that snaked towards the left-hand door looked as small as mice.

'That is the way in if you wish to get to the basilica and see the tomb of St Peter.'

A shudder of excitement ran through Galen at the thought of being so close to the remains of a man who once walked beside Jesus. He looked hopefully up at Alcuin who was also glowing with excitement.

'Of course, we must go in,' he said. 'How could we possibly come all the way here and turn away at the last moment?'

Piero nodded and said, 'I have seen it many times since I was a child, but it is one of the holiest of holy sites.'

'I can die happy if I can pray here,' Carbo said as they joined the back of an excited queue.

'While we wait, I can point out a few other interesting things,' Piero said. 'To the left, just behind and to the right of the basilica, is the Vatican Palace. We are currently standing on the Vatican Hill. To the right is an obelisk that was present at St Peter's martyrdom. They say Julius Caesar's ashes are sealed in the golden orb balanced on the tip of the obelisk. The land all around us is the burial ground of hundreds, if not thousands, of Christian martyrs, for this was where they were laid to rest after they were martyred in the circus.'

'How remarkable.'

Galen couldn't believe he was standing here. He'd never thought he'd go beyond the abbey after he left home. Thankfully, the queue moved quickly, so that now they were halfway up the shallow steps to the portico entrance.

'Maybe St Peter can perform a miracle for you,' Brother Piero said.

Galen tore his gaze away from the huge columns and intricate brickwork before him and said, 'Do you think that's likely?'

Piero waved his arm to encompass the ever-growing line of pilgrims, their heads bowed and their hands clasped before them in prayer. A fair few were on their knees, praying and rocking their bodies, shuffling forward as the line moved.

'Many people come here praying for a miracle.'

'I'm sure they do,' Galen murmured and cast a warning glance up at Carbo.

Thankfully, he wasn't paying attention to the conversation. His eyes were the size of plates as he took everything in.

'Didn't you come here on your first visit to Rome?' Alcuin asked, because he'd also caught Galen's eye and knew to be ready to step in should Carbo say anything about miracles.

'I didn't,' Carbo said. 'I remained at the abbey.'

'Well then, it was worth the extra trip, wasn't it?' Alcuin said.

Carbo nodded solemnly.

Galen agreed, especially as they went through the portico and into a large cloister. Ahead was a huge basilica of dimensions Galen wouldn't even be able to describe to people at home, for their imaginations would have no hope of picturing it. It was a fitting structure for the tomb of St Peter and the martyrs and subsequent popes, but it brought home to Galen the great importance of saints within his religion.

They had put this monumental building up to celebrate the glory of God and as a tribute to His most loyal supporters. Those were the people God blessed with wisdom and the ability to perform miracles.

No matter how Galen looked at it, he couldn't see how he fitted in. All he could do was write neatly. While any work done could be offered to God with prayers of thanks, his abilities were dwarfed by the lives of all the saints.

They also seemed to have such serenity and confidence, both of which he lacked. He had his suspicions that not all saints were as confident as they were portrayed, for often the stories about them were written centuries later. All the same, Galen didn't feel worthy.

'You are deep in thought,' Alcuin said, drawing Galen's attention back.

'Too many,' Galen said, waving his hand to dismiss them.

Since they weren't alone, Alcuin asked no more, but he knew his friend so well that Galen was sure Alcuin knew what he was thinking. How could he not when it had become something of an obsession? But, since the miracle that had brought Alcuin back to life, Alcuin, too, said less about miracles and saints.

'Perhaps you can give us one of your riddles to while away the time as we pass through this cloister,' Alcuin said.

Galen laughed, because his friend looked so hopeful.

'A riddle?' Brother Piero asked.

'The Anglo-Saxons seem to be very fond of riddles,' Brother Carbo said.

'I'll have to translate this into Latin on the spot, so it may not be very elegant,' Galen said, 'but do you want to try it?'

'Of course,' Alcuin said.

'Alright, here goes. This is a riddle that describes two things:

My hall is a place of sparkling sound. Although I am not loud.

Our paths flow together as ordained by the Lord.

Swifter and stronger am I at times. Constant and enduring is he.

Often I rest, but always he runs on.

All my life long, my home is with him.

Should we two be parted, death is my destiny.

What are we?'

'Tricky as ever,' Alcuin said with a pleased grin.

Carbo just shook his head.

'I have no hope of guessing that.'

Brother Piero looked intrigued.

'I didn't know you could also do riddles, Brother Galen.'

'It is a little entertainment of mine.'

'Is that what you have in your notebook?'

'There are a fair few riddles there, to be sure, but they are none of them original. I have collected them over the years.'

'Enough chat,' Alcuin said. 'I need to focus on the riddle and try to find the words that will act as my clues.'

It wasn't a bad way to while away the time, but no-one had guessed correctly by the time they shuffled into the massive basilica. It was dark inside and comprised one great hall with two broad corridors to either side. Around a hundred and fifty paces further in stood the main altar, at the end of a run of stairs. Tightly packed pilgrims surrounded it.

To be in the presence of a thousand years of history and these holy remains took Galen's breath away and he sank to his knees, thanking God for getting him this far. A susurration of prayer filled the space; every person as overwhelmed as Galen. Some were kneeling, others lying flat on the ground, their hands raised above their heads, palms upwards.

Galen bent his head and returned to his prayers. Thanks for getting so far, thanks for keeping everyone safe, and prayers for guidance on the next steps to take.

'For, you know, God, this is a vast and complicated city and I don't know the right thing to do.'

'Have you still not got the riddle?' Galen asked as the four monks sat perched upon a rocky outcrop above the river Tiber and ate their lunch.

His pain had subsided and he felt washed out after the emotional rush of being in St Peter's. It was like when he was a child and had a really long, cathartic cry. It wasn't like him to feel this emotional, but he didn't regret it.

'Of course I haven't given up, but your riddles are devilishly difficult,' Alcuin said as he bit off a sizeable chunk of bread.

'Would you like a clue?'

'No amount of clues will help me,' Carbo said.

As he'd not seemed interested in the riddle or bothered about trying to make a guess, Galen just smiled at him. Piero, on the other hand, had made a string of guesses during the morning, each one more outlandish than the next.

'Honestly, Brother Galen, I'll need more than a clue to figure this out. It appears you northern men have more cunning than a Venetian.'

'Is that a good thing?' Alcuin asked.

'Well...' Piero paused to consider. 'Let's just say that they are considered tricky and conniving.'

'I'm sure no more than any other people,' Galen said. 'But very well, I shall give you a clue. All you need is to look down.'

'Look down? Figuratively, or... I don't see how that helps,' Piero said, blinking at Galen.

Alcuin, though, got it and started laughing. 'Of course, the river, a sparkling, fluid thing.'

'Exactly,' Galen said. 'And the rest?'

'A companion to the river who would surely die if he was removed from it? Why, that has to be a fish.'

'Ah, yes, of course!' Piero said, snapping his fingers. 'It's so obvious once you know.'

'I still don't get it,' Carbo said, shaking his head.

Galen started to explain when a ferocious honking drowned his words. Coming towards them, wings flapping excitedly, was a flock of geese.

'Quick, the food, that's what they're after,' Piero said as he snatched up the loaf that had been lying on a cloth bag.

He shook the bag wildly, spreading crumbs all around, and the geese swooped in, honking and jostling to get at the remains.

'Back off, you vermin,' Carbo said, waving his staff about as he helped Galen to his feet.

Piero shouted at a young boy in that thick Roman dialect that Galen wished he could understand. The boy looked flushed but not really apologetic as he arrived, huffing, after the geese. He flicked a few of the animals' wings and necks with a thin willow switch, but it did nothing to restore order. Alcuin, in the meantime, had rescued their cheese and the flagon of wine and was shielding Galen from the rear. Fortunately, now that they were no longer in possession of the bread, the geese had lost interest in them.

'Piero, leave him be,' Alcuin shouted. 'We may as well head to our next stop.'

'Sorry about that, brothers,' Piero said as he hurried after them. 'Geese are the pride of Rome, for they've alerted us to many a sneak attack. They're better than guard dogs for detecting intruders. But they are also foul-tempered creatures who will happily pluck your eye out if you displease them.'

'We wouldn't want that,' Galen said, amused by the mixture of pride and embarrassment with which Piero spoke.

Piero flushed and said, 'It's the Basilica of Saints Cosmo and Damiano you want now, isn't it?'

Alcuin nodded. 'I've heard they have a particularly beautiful mosaic, and Galen wishes to pray to them for healing.'

'Well, it isn't far,' Piero said cheerfully.

'Did you know,' Alcuin said as they walked, 'that Cosmo and Damiano were both physicians? That's why the basilica is one for healing.'

'It always impresses me what a wide diversity of walks of life saints come from,' Galen said, trying to maintain a cheerful façade even though the tension of the upcoming secret meeting was making his stomach churn.

'Indeed,' Alcuin said. 'But even more interesting, and something I learned from Brother Iacopo, is that there was a famous Roman physician by the name of Claudius Galenus who used to teach there in the times when the basilica was a pagan temple.'

'I knew about him. My mother named me after him. She hoped I would be a healthy child, but I didn't know where he lived and worked.'

'It's a wondrous thing to find out these obscure connections. It's almost like piecing together a riddle.'

Galen nodded, glad of the distraction, for Piero's ideas of distance differed from Galen's as they'd walked for at least an hour and he winced with every step he took. By now, they had seen so many magnificent monuments that Galen had lost the ability to be astonished or distracted by them. The area they'd come to was far less busy. In fact, there were hardly any people at all, and they'd left the shops behind. Instead, there was just rough grass, shrubby bushes and an entire city's worth of decaying ancient buildings.

'All buildings of the ancient Romans,' Piero said, when he noticed Alcuin's interested gaze.

'They seem to have been very fond of great white columns,' Alcuin said. 'They produced enough of them.'

'Truly, this must have been a magnificent city a thousand years ago if those peoples could produce such a collection of buildings. I wonder what our people were doing so long ago,' Galen said, but only paying half his attention to the conversation for his anxiety about his upcoming meeting with the Theophylacti was overshadowing the rest.

'Who can say what our people were doing?' Alcuin said with a shrug.

'Not us, certainly. Our ancestors seem not to have committed anything to writing.'

'This is it,' Piero said as he came to a halt before a large circular building with a simple double door that stood ajar.

This space amongst the ruins was so quiet that the six well-armed men lounging in front seemed too blatant to Galen, who was sure they had accompanied the person he was due to meet. Piero and Carbo knew nothing about the meeting, of course, and Galen and Alcuin had discussed how Alcuin could distract them so that Galen could have his meeting in secret. Having what looked like guards at the door was not helpful.

Galen and Alcuin exchanged a dubious look, then Alcuin gave an infinitesimal shrug, grinned broadly and said, perhaps a bit too loudly, 'Well, shall we go inside?'

'Of course. It was quite a long walk,' Carbo said, glowering at Piero. 'It's tired Brother Galen out.'

'I'm afraid it has,' Galen said, leaning more heavily on Carbo than he would have liked, but that worked to his advantage for his and Alcuin's plan. 'I will rest in a quiet alcove while the rest of you explore the basilica.'

'As you wish, Brother,' Carbo said, patting Galen's hand as they stepped into the dim, chilly interior of the church.

At first glance it seemed empty, but on the left was a small side chapel and Galen spotted a figure kneeling in the deep shadows before the altar.

'I suppose because they have so many churches, the people don't use all of them as much as they might,' Alcuin said as he hurried forward to the apse to look at the mosaic. 'There it is,' he breathed, and his voice softened in wonder.

Lit as it was by only a pair of candles, it was difficult to make out the picture, but the gold mosaics gleamed and showed up a row of sheep encircling the bottom of an enormous image of the Second Coming.

Galen eased his arm out of Carbo's grip and indicated with a tilt of his chin that the big man should follow Alcuin. Piero had already hurried after him.

Then, his heart beating so fast he could feel it throbbing through his body, Galen made his way to the side chapel and the kneeling figure. As he got closer, he realised it was a woman, which reassured him. She was dressed all in black and swathed in a hooded black cape.

As Galen lowered himself to be near enough to speak softly, but not so close that they would touch, the woman turned her head and gazed at him, her face an expressionless mask. She was middle-aged, but slim and beautiful. What hair he could see, swept back under a veil, was still dark but with a few grey hairs starting to show. She had a strong nose and her eyes were large, dark and heavily lidded. She exuded power.

'Are you the one Fra' Martinus told me to meet?' she said, her voice rich and low.

Galen nodded.

'I was told you know what has happened to one of our family.'

'Sister Marozia,' Galen whispered, although he was scared to say the name in case it got him into trouble.

'I fear you don't have good news.'

'I'm sorry,' Galen said.

'It was to be expected when this meeting was arranged so carefully. I am Lady Chedira.'

'Brother Galen of Yarmwick.'

Galen remembered that Fra' Martinus had said that if he was to get a favour in return he had to identify himself. He'd have felt more at ease to remain anonymous. The woman nodded, and looked like she was committing his name to memory.

'So, tell me, what do you know?'

'It's a long story,' Galen said and told her about how Marozia and her followers had been massacred and their bodies disposed of.

Lady Chedira kept her head bowed, but her body tensed and her hands, clasped before her, grew tighter and tighter.

'They went to such an extent?' she said when Galen finished. Her face was hard, her dark brows drawn together.

Galen wished he could give her some words of comfort, but he couldn't think of any.

'Do you know who did it?' Lady Chedira asked.

'I don't know for certain,' Galen said and wondered whether he should mention this additional information at all. But he wanted answers too, and he felt Marozia deserved justice, not oblivion. 'There was a monk in Sister Marozia's company, one Brother Bartolo. He survived the attack, although he was badly injured. He told us that the pope ordered him to follow and report back on Sister Marozia's activities.'

'Where is that monk now?'

'We helped him get to Rome but, after that, I don't know where he went.'

'He was badly injured, you say?'

Galen nodded.

'And he isn't at San Agato?'

'Definitely not.'

'I must find him.'

'His injuries were severe. I doubt he is still alive,' Galen said and wondered yet again whether he should at least have tried laying his hands on Bartolo to see what God wished to do. It was too late for that now, though. 'Do you think the pope was involved?'

'The current pope works hand in glove with the emperor. Everything he does is to strengthen his cousin's hold on power. That includes thousands of dispensations for monasteries across the empire.'

'Bribes?'

'Of course. Keep them fat and happy and monks won't cause trouble. But the pope also threatened to excommunicate Robert II of France and forced him to abandon his wife. That was purely to bring the man to heel for the emperor. Saint Nilus was right - their cruelty will bring them down.'

Galen wondered whether that was true. He'd seen many vicious men live happily into old age.

Lady Chedira gave a sigh that seemed to wash the tension from her body. 'You have been a great help to our house. So now we owe you a favour. I understand you wish to see the pope.'

Galen blinked at her in surprise.

'You would do that for me, even knowing what you know now?'

'Liking someone, or even plotting vengeance on someone, does not preclude you from their company. Although the present pope and emperor have kept my family at arm's length, I can still arrange an audience for you, if that is what you wish.'

Galen couldn't decide. The pope seemed less and less like the kind of person who could give him the answers he needed. He didn't even want to tell the pope that he might be a saint. He suspected that if word of what had happened to him reached the pope, it might make life even more complicated.

'Thank you for the offer. I will have to think about it.'

'That would probably be for the best. Fra' Martinus can send us a message once you decide,' Lady Chedira said, then she rose to her feet and sailed off.

Galen spent the time in prayer, running over what had been said and what it meant. Then he headed to Alcuin and Piero. Carbo was on his knees in the middle of the church, his hood pulled up and his head bowed in prayer. Alcuin had picked up one of the candles and held it up so that he could make out more of the astonishing image.

'Look at those colours, Galen!' he said at his approach. 'And the way the artist could make the folds on their gowns look so realistic, and their faces, oh their faces are perfect!'

Galen gazed up at the larger-than-life mosaic figures surrounded by a more intense blue than paint could achieve.

'It is exquisite.'

'It is indeed,' Alcuin said as he looked about for more light, spotted a couple more candles and lit them with the one he was holding.

Galen wondered whether the local priest might appear at any moment to admonish Alcuin for wasting his candles, but his friend looked so happy he said nothing, especially as Piero seemed to be enjoying himself too and learning a great deal. So Galen stepped back, admired the art and tried to relax under the glow of Alcuin and Piero's enthusiasm.

Chapter 10

Aside from the ever increasing cold and the shorter days, little changed and Galen grew restless. He worried they weren't doing anything to see the pope, then worried again that he should avoid the pope.

In addition, Fra' Martinus made him nervous and he didn't dare approach him to find out what he was doing to help Alcuin and Galen fulfil Bishop Sigburt's final request. He didn't want another awkward debate with the man either. So all he could do was live day to day.

This morning, like every morning, he pulled his cowl on while still under his blanket, which was blessedly warm. Then he got up, put on his day shoes and hurried to the latrines, before heading, with Alcuin, to the church for Prime.

'The pope's back.'

Galen heard the words whispered behind him as he and Alcuin headed across the cloister. He turned around to ask the speaker how he knew, but in the dim light of dawn with the line of monks behind him, all with their hoods pulled up, he had no hope of telling who had spoken.

'Did you hear that?' Galen whispered to Alcuin.

'Hear what?'

'The pope's back.'

'That's good.'

Alcuin pushed his hood back, looking about, then his face lit up so Galen knew he'd spotted Carbo. The big man always got to the church before them and kept the seats beside him free.

'The pope's back,' Carbo mouthed, the moment Galen and Alcuin drew near.

Galen wanted to know more, but talk wasn't allowed within the church and there was an expectant hush as the last few monks arrived and the prayers commenced. Brother Stefano led them this morning. He was the oldest monk at the abbey that Brother Piero had told Galen about. His voice was weak and cracked. In the quiet of the vast church it echoed off the stone walls and sounded like wind through reeds.

Galen pushed away all the questions about the pope and when they might see him and focused on his prayers. He became so lost in contemplation of God that the silence that fell as the notes of the last prayer dissipated into the dark of the church startled him.

'So, what should we do about the pope?' Alcuin said the moment he and Galen were clear of the church with Carbo looming behind them.

'I don't know,' Galen said. 'If we have to wait for Fra' Martinus to arrange an audience I'm certain it won't be today.'

'The pope will deliver a mass at St John Lateran cathedral today,' Carbo said.

'You are well informed,' Alcuin said.

'Well, I need him to bless various unguents and salves for my monastery.'

'Oh yes, of course. That was why you came to Rome, after all.'

'That was what my fra' came up with as an excuse and it's true, even if it's not the most important reason.'

'So... do you have some salves?' Galen asked as they stepped out of the shadow of the church into blessedly warm winter sunshine.

The cloister was echoing with the chatter from the ever increasing crowds of monks emerging from the church. It was Sunday, a day of rest and peaceful contemplation, and everyone was getting their conversation done before they entered a period of silence.

'I brought some salves and unguents we made at home, and the infirmarius here has been kind enough to give me a bit more,' Carbo said.

'So how will you get the pope's blessing?'

'I was told to hold everything up towards the pope when he gives the final blessing at the end of the mass.'

'That would do the trick. Were you thinking of going today?'

'Why not? The sooner the better.'

'Should we go along too?' Alcuin asked.

Galen's heartbeat quickened as a wave of anxiety washed over him.

'Do you think... do you think we should try to meet the pope ourselves? Is that wise?'

'Ah, no, I wasn't thinking that. If we managed that I'd call it a miracle. A big one.'

'It would also offend our host.'

A part of Galen wished he could just meet the pope and get the whole thing over and done with. He felt like he was holding his breath in Rome. But if they completed their mission then at least he could focus on his translations.

'We wouldn't want to displease our host,' Alcuin said. 'But going out with Carbo will surely keep us safe.'

'Well… yes, then let's do that… at least we'll see a bit more of Rome as well.'

'Do you want to see more of Rome?' Alcuin said, giving Galen a knowing grin.

'It was the centre of learning for a very long time. It has many marvels.'

'And you have a taste for marvels, don't you? Not to mention all the holy sites we can visit.'

It made Galen happy that Alcuin knew him so well.

'It might be the only chance we get, Alcuin, especially if we're leaving in the spring.'

'Only if we've seen the pope by then.'

'Surely it can't take that long?' Galen said, feeling foolish for letting slip his hopes of when they'd be heading home.

'Well, I don't know,' Alcuin said, but as he obviously didn't want to dash Galen's mood, he let the matter drop.

'Are you sure you're up for it, Brother Galen?' Carbo asked. 'You still don't look fully recovered.'

'I'll be fine,' Galen said. 'I'm a little more robust than I was. If I can walk all the way from Al-Andalus, I can go the short distance to St John Lateran.'

'A little more robust? Well… if you say so. And I will keep you safe from bandits and soldiers at least.'

'They didn't seem such a great danger the last time we went out.'

'Travelers hardly notice the dangers around them, for they don't know what to look out for. Then later they'll bless themselves and say the place was perfectly safe, when they actually just got lucky. Believe me, there are thieves in this city who'd sooner knock you out than talk to you because it's less fuss. All it will take is one swift crack to your skull and you'd be dead.'

'But I have nothing of value.'

'They won't know that till after they've hit you over the head. Besides, that cloak of yours is nice, very nice indeed. They'd rob you just to get their hands on it, especially now that it's winter.'

'When the sun is shining, the day is warmer here,' Alcuin said. 'In fact, I think their winters overall are milder than in Enga-lond.'

'I've heard that it doesn't get quite as cold here as in my home and yours, but a good cloak is a good cloak, no matter where you are.'

'I'm sure with you accompanying us we'll be fine,' Galen said, giving Carbo his most encouraging smile.

The potential dangers they might face intimidated him, but considering all he and Alcuin had gone through to reach Rome, he felt less worried than he might have at the start of the journey.

'Very well, we'll go together. Let me get some food from the kitchen, for we'll not be back in time for dinner.'

'Do you know the way?' Alcuin asked.

'Ah... no, but I'm sure the porter and the people of Rome will be able to point us in the right direction.'

'I'm not so sure about that,' Alcuin murmured as Carbo hurried off to the kitchen. 'Perhaps we can get Brother Piero to show us around again.'

Galen nodded and looked for Piero. He was on the other side of the cloister, being harangued by an older man. Galen had only been mentoring the lad for a few weeks, but he already felt protective towards him and took a couple of steps in his direction before he realised what he was doing. Then took a deep breath to fortify himself and hurried over.

'I am working hard, Brother Antonius. I give you my word,' Brother Piero was saying.

He sounded so miserable and looked so browbeaten that Galen pushed down his rising anxiety to approach such a fierce man. He had a ruddy complexion and with the yellow morning sun picking out the auburn in his hair, it added to his fiery look.

'I know you, Piero. You were forever slipping off to play truant rather than doing your work. It will do you no good to lie to me.'

'But he isn't lying,' Galen said, and it came out softer than he'd intended.

'Who are you to tell me what my former novice is like? You don't even belong in this abbey,' the man snapped, leaning menacingly towards Galen.

He took a hasty step back and bumped into Alcuin who'd hurried after him and was now scowling back at the man.

'Who exactly are you?' Alcuin asked at his icy, imperious best.

'I am Brother Antonius, the master of the boys.'

'But Brother Piero is no longer under your instruction, is he?'

'Well, no, but I still feel a sense of duty towards him.'

'You should also have trust in him,' Galen said with a frightened tremor in his voice. 'Piero has been working under me, and I have found nothing to be disappointed with in him. His work is excellent.'

'Give him time,' Brother Antonius said. 'He often starts off well.'

'I'm sure he'll do fine,' Galen said, smiling encouragingly up at Piero.

It surprised him to see gratitude in the young man's eyes.

'Hah!' the master of the boys said and put his hands on his hips.

It was obvious he would not be convinced, and Alcuin seemed to have decided the same thing.

He turned away from Brother Antonius and said, 'We have need of you again, Brother Piero. Fancy going out with us into Rome?'

'Oh, yes, I'd like that,' Piero said, glancing back at Brother Antonius who was chewing his lips in impotent fury.

'Excellent! This time we need you to show us the way to the cathedral of St John Lateran.'

'I'd be honoured,' Piero said, his face lighting up. 'I can show you some of the other sights along the way as well.'

'We'd like that,' Alcuin said and put both his arms out to encompass Galen and Piero and shepherd them away while giving Brother Antonius a smiling nod of farewell.

It was typical Alcuin, Galen thought. He was so good at managing people.

This time the quartet of monks headed south east past the shops and along the lane Galen suspected led back to the Basilica of Saints Cosmo and Damiano. It was hard to be sure because Rome was a maze and many of the buildings looked similar. The churches and massive towers of the warring barons provided landmarks, but it was still an alien landscape for an outsider.

Then Piero led them out into the wide expanse of ruins, and Galen recognised the basilica where he'd met Lady Chedira. They walked past that church and further into the ruins. They rounded a particularly large pile of stones and Galen stopped dead.

Ahead of them was an extraordinary, massive, circular building. He hadn't even thought that Rome still had the power to surprise him, but this was the most astonishing sight so far. He tilted his head back and looked up and up at the wide, white-stoned circumference.

'What is this?'

'Looks to me like a great Roman theatre,' Carbo said. 'They certainly knew how to build big, those ancients.'

'Big?!' Galen gasped. 'That theatre would hold all the inhabitants of Lundenburh, and its walls are five times higher than most city walls.'

'It's the Colosseum,' Pietro said. 'The ancient citizens of Rome watched entertainments here.'

Galen's eyes widened all the more as he said, 'What manner of entertainment could they possibly see in a place so vast?'

'Probably something barbaric, like martyring Christians,' Carbo said.

'They were violent, but also a very great people. They gave us Latin, after all.'

'Yes, martyring Christians happened there,' Piero said, 'but also other things. My father told me they would fill the

Colosseum stage with water and hold sea battles in there with full-sized ships.'

Galen and Alcuin stared at him in amazement.

'How is that even possible?'

Galen might have thought it was a fanciful tale told by an imaginative adolescent, but the fact that his father had told Piero this tale made him wonder whether it might not be true.

'They're all gone now,' Alcuin said, 'and we'd best get a move on if we're to reach St John Lateran in time.'

Galen could barely tear his eyes away from the Colosseum, but he also wished they could stop a while and rest because the pain in his guts had increased. At the same time, he didn't want to delay his companions and have Carbo miss out on the pope's blessing for his unguents.

The ground gave a thud, like something extremely heavy had dropped right beside Galen, that made him jump.

'What was that?' Carbo asked, crossing himself.

'An earth tremor,' Piero said and tilted his head, listening intently.

'Is this something we should be worried about?' Alcuin asked.

'It might be nothing, or it might presage a larger quake,' Piero said, looking tense. 'May I suggest we go up the Palatine Hill and wait for a bit?'

'Why up the hill?' Carbo asked, looking up at a grass- and weed-covered not very tall hill strewn with the massive blocks of fallen buildings and where Roman columns and more complete ruins poked out of the ground.

'Well... it's away from any major buildings, so it should be safe, and we'll be able to see more of Rome and what's

going on. If it all looks quiet, we can give it an hour or so
and then continue on our way.'

'I would be grateful for the rest,' Galen murmured, for
he knew that would decide Alcuin and Carbo on this
plan.

He also needed to calm down. He knew nothing about
earthquakes and feeling the earth thump had unsettled
him.

'Well, if we're going to stop, we may as well have our
food,' Alcuin said cheerfully.

It sounded a bit forced to Galen.

'Very well,' Carbo said, turning to the path that took
them up the hill. 'Are earthquakes a frequent occurrence
in Rome? I didn't experience one the last time I was here.'

'They aren't very common.' Piero led them to a wide
marble block that looked like it had formed part of a porch
long ago. A young elm tree had grown up through a crack,
its roots now merged with the shattered stone, while
its bare fishbone pattern of branches cast a lattice-like
shadow on the stone. 'But they happen now and then.
There once was a church called Santa Maria Antiqua that
was buried in an earthquake. One minute it was above
ground, the next it was swallowed whole, never to be seen
again.'

'Dear God, have mercy on us,' Carbo said, crossing
himself three times in quick succession before he helped
Galen to lower himself onto the marble base.

Galen supposed he had good reason to be afraid. He was
a big, strong man, but even his strength was meaningless
when the earth shook. It added to Galen's unease. Then
he pushed it away and looked around for distraction. This
was easily found since Rome was such a strange city.

'How can this be so empty when we are in the middle of Rome?' Galen asked, looking across the hill down to the Colosseum that was filled with nothing but rough grass.

Further away was a row of low stone houses with fenced off vegetable plots. The fencing made sense because the only life visible here was a man chasing an agitated herd of pigs.

'Rome once had many more people,' Piero said, swinging his legs back and forth on the edge of the porch. 'During the time of the ancient Romans, it is said there were more than a million people living here.'

'Nonsense!' Carbo said on a snort as he handed the sling bag he'd been carrying to Alcuin who reached inside and pulled out a loaf of bread.

'It could be possible,' Galen said. 'Look at the size of this place, and it has two formidable city walls, an inner one that encompasses a space way larger than Lundenburh and an outer one that is even bigger. Then there's all these ruins. Even now, when people are picking them apart to use the stone and bricks to make new buildings, there are still plenty left.'

'Hmm,' Carbo grunted, clearly not in agreement but equally not wishing to argue with Galen.

It made Galen feel guilty, for he was sure he only got this respect from Carbo because he thought him a saint.

'Enough of that,' Alcuin said cheerfully, 'let's pray and then eat.'

'Brother Galen can lead the prayer,' Carbo said.

It embarrassed Galen that nobody challenged the big man. So he bowed his head and began the prayers.

'Always so thoughtful,' Alcuin murmured as Galen finished.

Then Alcuin sliced up the bread and the cheese and waved for everyone to help themselves.

As always, Carbo waited until Galen had taken a slice of cheese before diving in. Carbo made himself a sandwich of the bread and cheese, then dusted a section of the stone clean and placed a slice of bread beside Galen, beaming at him and gesturing that he should eat. Galen didn't have the appetite for it but nodded his thanks anyway. Food was never particularly appealing when he was in pain.

'Have some of the wine,' Alcuin said as he handed over the flagon, for he knew how Galen was in these circumstances. 'It's spiced.'

Galen took a sip out of gratitude for Alcuin's attention rather than because he was thirsty. Then he broke off a corner of the cheese and nibbled at it.

'Brother Iacopo mentioned a living saint, one Nilus of Rossano. Do you know anything about him, Brother Piero?'

It had surprised Galen at the time of the conversation in the scriptorium to hear of a living saint and of his influence over the pope and the emperor, but it took some courage for him to bring up the question. Alcuin must have thought so too as his eyebrow rose, but he kept his attention focused on his lunch and took a big bite of bread and cheese.

'There are any number of saints in Rome, many self-proclaimed,' Piero said with an uninterested shrug. 'But Nilus of Rossano, or Nilus the Younger, as he is often called, is a real saint. Only he isn't based in Rome but in Rossano, south of here.'

'Is he a young man?' Alcuin asked.

'Oh no, he's very old. I saw him at the end of the war last year when he came to plead for his friend who had been the anti-pope. He has a long, flowing white beard.'

'Ah, so they were friends,' Carbo said. 'The anti-pope couldn't have been that bad if he was friends with a saint.'

'Everyone is friends with at least one saint in Rome,' Piero said with a dismissive shrug.

It was such a surprising comment that it struck Galen rather forcibly. Was sainthood not as special as he'd assumed?

'All the same,' Piero continued, 'Saint Nilus is a genuine saint, of that I am sure. He also delivered a prophecy to the pope and the emperor.'

'What did he say?' Alcuin asked, his half-eaten lunch forgotten with Piero's pronouncement.

'He said: the curse of heaven sooner or later would affect the cruel hearts of the pope and the emperor.'

The ground shook, trembling as if from the words. His slice of cheese slipped from Galen's fingers and he clutched at the marble that shivered under his touch like a terrified animal.

'Lord have mercy on our souls,' Carbo muttered and went back to crossing himself.

'This is more troubling,' Piero said, scanning the city.

The pigs were snorting with alarm, dogs were howling in the distance and people had run from their homes dragging children and livestock, all heading to the open space around the Colosseum.

'What should we do now? Return to San Agato?' Galen asked, his heart filled with foreboding.

'During an earthquake it's best to stay out in the open where no collapsing building can bury you. Earthquakes are the only time the monks of San Agato are allowed to leave the abbey. If you went back now, aside from fighting against the flow of people leaving the built-up areas, you'd find the abbey deserted.'

'But where will they all have gone?'

'They are most likely heading our way,' Piero said.

'And then what?'

'They will wait and see. If nothing happens within the next couple of hours, the people will return to their homes.'

CHapter 11

No further tremors shook the ground, but Galen felt so disturbed by the experience that he couldn't focus on much and spent the time praying. His companions did the same. Alcuin and Piero sat opposite Galen, heads bowed, their lips moving. Carbo had found himself a patch of short mown grass and was kneeling in the sun, praying out loud for deliverance.

Most of the people who had come out into the open stayed further down the hill, but their chatter carried up the mountain. The voices were sharp and held a note of fear. The women spoke more softly. A lot of babies and children were crying. Now and then an uneasy, overloud laugh punctuated the din, a goat gave an annoyed bleat, or the flocks of geese set to honking. But as the time passed, the nervousness of the people subsided. Then, one by one or in groups, they slipped back home.

'What would you like to do now, brothers?' Piero asked. 'Return to San Agato or continue on?'

'Do you think the pope will still hold his mass?' Alcuin asked.

'I'm sure he will. He will thank God for sparing us and pray to Him to continue His protection.'

'Then I say we go on,' Carbo said. 'If Brother Galen is up to it.'

Everyone turned to Galen, and he shrank under their examination. He was feeling more shaky than expected and was unsure if it was merely exhaustion or shock or a combination of the two. He was also filled with foreboding, which he put down to nerves. In his state it was better to be distracted and, what was more, he didn't want to get in the way of Carbo's mission.

'Let's continue.'

'Alright then.'

Piero hopped off his marble perch and headed downhill towards the inner wall of the city. They merged with the last few stragglers returning to the more built-up areas and passed a number more churches, many of them with the tall, square campanili that Galen had come to view as a symbol of Rome.

At each of the churches there were groups of people standing outside praying. Galen guessed they had not gone inside for fear of further earthquakes and collapse. He also suspected that there were more people at prayer than on a normal day.

As they walked, Galen's pain increased until he felt nauseous and dizzy. He was desperate to sit and catch his breath, but he held off, determined to make it to the next corner and then the next, convinced they must be near the pope's palace.

Finally, they reached the inner wall of the city. Piero led them through the archway of an open gate and across a smelly river that at one time may have formed a moat to the wall, but was now little more than an open sewer.

'Here we are,' Piero said, waving his arm to encompass a vast square the likes of which Galen had never seen before.

At the far end was a gigantic and austere basilica. Clustered around it was a palace and one of the tallest bell towers Galen had yet seen, with a sharp triangular roof. There were hundreds of people in this square and more monks and priests than before the other churches. There were also groups of ragged people: some looked like beggars, some were most likely pilgrims, and some may have been the starving farmers Marozia had spoken of. Around them, like stone guards, was an astonishing collection of sculptures, including a massive bronze foot and a matching bronze head that seemed like stuff from a nightmare, for they made no sense.

'The oldest church in Rome, and the seat of the bishop of Rome,' Piero said. 'St John Lateran.'

Galen was exhausted now, the world fading in and out, and he leaned more heavily on Carbo, uncertain he could stand without support.

'It's an enormous building,' Carbo said. 'But not the most beautiful we've seen so far.'

'That's probably because it's so old,' Piero said.

Alcuin nodded as he took in the palace, with its many storeys, and the sculptures. It didn't surprise Galen that his friend's artistic eye was drawn to the sculptures.

'It's going to be quite a job getting through all those people and into the church,' Alcuin said as he turned back to his friend.

Galen barely heard him. Dread washed over him as the world shook once more and the sky over the palace turned blood-red and filled with billowing storm clouds that blotted out the weak sun. It seemed it would swallow the whole world.

'I can't go in there,' Galen said as fear squeezed a fist about his chest, depriving him of breath. 'I have to get away!'

'Galen, what's wrong?' Alcuin asked.

'The... the ground shook, and the sky... the sky turned red,' Galen said, looking up at what was a clear sky with just a few dots of clouds again.

'You're obviously not feeling well,' Alcuin said. 'There was no earthquake just now.'

'All the same,' Galen said.

'It would be better to go into the church and gather yourself,' Alcuin said, 'rather than trying to walk back in your current condition.'

Galen felt frozen to the spot with fear and indecision. He'd never had such an intense feeling of repulsion in his life, certainly not over going into a church. Carbo and Piero were watching him in alarm, while Alcuin was doing his best to project a confident calm.

'I can go in myself and get my unguents blessed,' Carbo said. 'You stay out here and rest, Brother Galen.'

'Yes,' Galen said, already filled with doubt over whether he was doing the right thing, but his legs simply wouldn't carry him further.

Alcuin gave him an encouraging smile that looked more dubious than usual and reflected how worried he was.

'Clear the way, clear the way for the pope,' a voice shouted from behind them.

Carbo stepped aside, dragging everyone with him, then dropped to his knees, like everyone else. A procession of priests walked past, chanting prayers. Each man carried a thurible filled with burning incense whose smoke was whipped away in the wind.

Behind them, wearing robes of white and gold, walked a pale-looking young man. On his head was a tall bulbous hat bearing three crowns, one stacked above the other, also in white and gold, that reminded Galen of a beehive. In the man's right hand was a curved shepherd's staff, the top of which was also made from gold. He was staring straight ahead.

Alcuin was trying his best to help Galen kneel while also keeping his head bowed. But Galen couldn't bring himself to do this either. He was still standing as the pope passed, and he turned to stare at Galen from blank, uninterested, pale grey eyes.

It's true, Galen thought. This man will reap what he has sown. Then a powerful spasm seized Galen. He doubled over, wrenching himself out of Alcuin's grip, and collapsed.

'Galen!' Alcuin shouted. He wrapped his arms around Galen's waist and lifted him onto his knees.

Galen coughed, and bright red blood splattered onto the cobbles.

'Galen, my God, what's wrong?!' Alcuin cried.

'No time to ask,' Carbo said as he swept Galen into his arms and took off at a run. 'We have to get him to the infirmarius!'

Alcuin ran after the big man, calling for to him to go slower, while Piero ran ahead shouting for people to clear the way. Alcuin was terrified for Galen and worried about the damage Carbo might do if he shook Galen too much with his pounding steps. Then his vision blurred and a rainbow of colours danced before his eyes then trailed away and wrapped itself around the edge of a building which detached itself and drifted off.

Alcuin stopped, stunned by this sight, and grabbed on to the wall to maintain his balance. The wall rippled under his hand and he snatched it away and gazed in horror as the bricks buckled and it seemed something flowed away under what should have been a solid edifice.

Was this another earthquake?

Saliva filled his mouth as nausea welled up from his stomach. He swallowed, desperately trying to keep everything down, but it was to no avail. He collapsed to his knees as his lunch came swirling up his gullet and he spewed his guts out. Over and over, gasping for breath between the beast-like spasms that wracked his body, till finally, finally, it stopped.

Alcuin shook from the tremendous effort and his stomach ached, but he didn't have time to worry about himself. He staggered after Carbo's fast-vanishing bulk laden with his inert bundle.

Piero was at the head of their breathless procession when they arrived at the abbey. He jangled the bell and then, without waiting, pushed the door open.

It surprised Alcuin that it wasn't locked, but Carbo just charged through, bellowing, 'I need the infirmarius!'

But the reception room and the courtyard were eerily silent, with not a soul about. That was wrong, the place was always busy. With so many monks it was inevitable that everywhere felt crowded. Here there was nobody.

'Hello?' Carbo shouted. 'Is anybody here?'

'The infirmary is this way,' Piero said, propping himself up against a side door to Alcuin's right.

Piero also looked pale, but that may have been due to the unaccustomed exercise. No reply came in response to Carbo's bellowing, and Alcuin was filled with foreboding. A motion caught the periphery of his vision and he swung round to speak to the person, but they slipped away. He swung back as he caught yet another movement and his mouth dropped open in amazement. A gargoyle blinked at him, poised halfway down the wall.

'No!' he gasped.

'What's going on?' Carbo asked.

At first Alcuin thought the question was directed at him, but when he looked up at the big man, his eyes were also wide and staring and a dribble of spit had slipped from his mouth and was heading for the tip of his chin.

'Carbo, can you hear me?'

'So many colours!' Carbo mumbled, his eyes staring unseeingly ahead of him. 'There are rainbows everywhere.'

That was what he'd experienced, so Alcuin said, 'Carbo, give me Galen.'

'What?'

'Hand Galen to me!' Alcuin said, infusing his voice with every ounce of authority he had.

'I have to protect him.'

'Now!' Alcuin shouted.

Carbo staggered sideways, then thrust Galen into Alcuin's arms. He couldn't hold him as Carbo had but hung on to him and tried to keep him from slipping to the floor.

Carbo's face went white. He moaned, bent over double and heaved up his lunch. It was what Alcuin expected, the reason he'd taken Galen from the big man. At the same time, Piero gave a strangled grunt and also threw up.

'Do you feel better?' Alcuin asked, directing the question to both men after what felt like an age of desperate waiting.

Carbo groaned but said, 'What happened?'

'It must have been something we ate. It hit Galen first. Remember, he also saw something at the palace. Then I saw strange visions and so did you.'

'Maybe it's a sign. Maybe the end of the world is upon us,' Carbo said, his eyes starting and panic-stricken.

'No, Carbo! Listen, we're ill, that's all, and we need to get Galen to the infirmarius.'

'This way,' Piero said, waving his arm as if that would get them to move faster.

'I'll take him,' Carbo said. 'He's too heavy for you.'

'Are you up to it?'

'I'm shaky, but I'll bet no worse than you. And Brother Galen weighs little more than a child. He's easy to carry.'

'I fear his frailty has made him more susceptible to whatever affected us.'

Carbo nodded, hoisted Galen back into his arms and, stepping over Piero's vomit that had spattered across the entrance, headed into the dark corridor and down to a large hall-like hospital.

The place was heaving with people, some lying still, pale and feverish, others writhing in the beds crying. Alcuin made his way to Brother Nicolaus, the infirmarius and the one man Alcuin had made sure he could identify from the first day of their stay in the abbey.

'We have a gravely ill man here. Can you look after him?'

'He'll have to wait his turn,' Brother Nicolaus said, distracted by the man he was trying to treat who was frothing at the mouth.

'He is more gravely affected than most. He threw up blood,' Alcuin said, unwilling to wait.

'Where is he?'

'Here,' Carbo said, holding Galen's still form out to the infirmarius.

'Hmmm,' the man murmured, his dispassionate gaze taking in where a trickle of blood had slipped out of Galen's mouth and down the side of his face. 'Alright, you'd better find him a bed.'

'Doesn't look like there is one,' Carbo said, surveying the room from his superior height.

'Then take someone else out of their bed. Some of them can sit on the floor. It won't harm them.'

That alarmed Alcuin. Was Galen's condition so bad he could commandeer a bed for him?

Carbo had no compunction about it.

He found a man who looked for all the world like he was merely resting and said, 'You, out! We need this bed for someone really sick.'

The man looked like he was going to argue until he opened his eyes and saw Carbo's massive frame. He reluctantly hauled himself out of the bed and, muttering profanities under his breath, moved away.

'You go to the chapel and pray forgiveness for your foul tongue,' Carbo snapped as he lowered Galen onto the bed.

'Get him on his side,' Alcuin said.

'Everyone else is lying flat on their backs.'

'I know, but it would be better if you place him on his side.'

Whilst Carbo carefully rolled Galen over, Alcuin checked, as surreptitiously as possible, to see whether Galen had started to bleed. To his relief, it appeared not, but he would have to keep his eye on that. He was determined not to mention Galen's other injuries to anyone in this monastery unless it was absolutely necessary.

Then he looked around for Piero. It would have been useful to have his support too, but Brother Nicolaus had already claimed Piero's strong, young arms, and he was currently holding down another patient thrashing about in a bed.

'It is a judgement,' a thin old voice cried. 'A judgement on us all as we approach a new millennium!'

Carbo and Alcuin looked up to see the ancient Brother Stefano. His clothes were awry and he was propped up on his walking stick. His pronouncement produced an instant effect. Monks crossed themselves and some fell to the floor, prostrating themselves in prayer.

'Lo, for the millennium is nearly upon us and we are all afflicted by visions. It is a sign. Repent, repent!'

'That's enough, Stefano!' Fra' Martinus said as he stalked into the infirmary, supported by a young monk. 'I will not have you sowing panic in my abbey.'

'How can you deny the evidence of your own eyes? First the earthquakes and now this. See how your people suffer.'

'They suffer because they all ate bad bread,' Fra' Martinus said, and his voice was heavy with disdain. 'I have this minute ordered our cellarer to get rid of all the flour that batch of bread was baked from. On my orders he has also sent a lay brother to the merchant who sold us the flour to find out whether any of his other customers are suffering the way we are.'

'No! There were visions,' Brother Stefano said, but his voice sounded weaker and more petulant now.

'Everyone who ate the bread had visions. It was the bad flour.'

'It may still hold a truth.'

'Perhaps, but which one of the diverse visions each man had would you say held a universal truth, and which are seeds of doubt sown by the devil? Best not to trust any of them. Now go back to your bed, my old friend. You shouldn't strain yourself.'

'I'd say that's good advice for Fra' Martinus too,' Carbo whispered to Alcuin, who nodded.

The fra', though, had other ideas. He walked between the rows of beds looking like death come amongst them, as he examined his monks and the people who'd come to the abbey for succour.

Fra' Martinus came to a stop before Galen's bed and said, 'He doesn't look well.'

'I fear, because of his frailty, this poisonous bread has affected him more than the rest of us,' Alcuin said.

'Indeed. I myself was fortunate I only partook of the pottage today or I may well have been carried off. You watch over him. Make sure he pulls through.'

CHAPTER 12

The effects of the bread, though severe for many, carried off none in the infirmary. Finally, the only one left in the hospital was Galen. Despite regaining consciousness, Galen was so wracked by fever that he didn't know anyone and cried out for his mother in his pain.

Alcuin and Carbo remained by his side nursing him and trying to keep him calm, although Alcuin wasn't sure whether he preferred it when Galen was lost to them in a deep, death-like sleep, or when he thrashed about, unable to get comfortable. On balance, he decided, he preferred the active phase of the illness, for then he at least knew his friend was still alive.

Alcuin was sitting in the near total darkness of the infirmary, so tired that the flickering of a lone candle held his gaze with a mesmeric power, when he heard Galen gasp in air. His gaze dropped immediately to inspect his friend and found himself being watched.

'Alcuin? Alcuin, is that you?'

'Yes, yes, it's me. Thank God you know me.'

'Why wouldn't I know you?' Galen said, his voice thick and slurred by fever-induced weakness.

'You've been ill for rather a long time.'

'What happened? How did I land up here? I don't remember,' Galen said, getting agitated as he realised he didn't know where he was.

'It's alright, keep calm,' Alcuin said in his level voice. 'You're in the abbey hospital. We all ate some poisoned bread and it affected us rather badly.'

'You?'

'Me too, for a while. But I'm better now.'

'There's nobody here but you and me. Where is everybody? Why is it so dark?'

'Hush now, don't get worked up else you'll bring on the fever again,' Alcuin said as he lifted Galen into a sitting position, propped him up with a couple of pillows and held the bowl of gruel he had waiting to his lips. 'Have a sip. You need to build up your strength.'

'But where is everybody?'

'They're in the church. Don't worry about them.'

'All of them, all in the church?' Galen said. 'What time is it?'

'I'd say it's nearly midnight.'

'What are they doing in church at midnight? What's wrong?' Galen said, working himself into a state.

'It's New Year's Eve, that's all,' Alcuin said as calmly as he could, although he was feeling nervous. 'They're praying for a prosperous new year without too many disasters.'

'Too many disasters?'

'Well, it will be the year of our Lord 999, and only one year to the millennium now.'

'Oh,' Galen said as he sank back into his pillows.

It struck Alcuin that Galen had never feared the millennium as the rest of them did. In fact, he'd always seemed supremely indifferent. Alcuin wondered why, but filed the thought away for another time. Galen was in no condition for deep thought and Alcuin didn't want to bring on a brain fever by pushing him.

'I had a vision, Alcuin.'

'When?' Alcuin said, coming back from his thoughts.

'It seems like a long time ago, but also present all the time. Whenever I close my eyes I see disaster looming over the pope's palace. Alcuin, he's going to die!' Galen said as a shudder ran through him.

'No, he isn't, don't worry,' Alcuin said, back to his calm, almost disinterested voice.

He'd long since learned that it worked like a balm on Galen's nerves. Any sign of sympathy from him put Galen instantly into a panic, fearing what was going on and why people were keeping it from him.

'The bad bread we ate gave us all visions. I saw the walls of a house come alive and gargoyles running down them, and Carbo saw rainbows over the abbey.'

'No,' Galen said. 'The pope is going to die. Someone should warn him.'

'I will see to it. I'll tell Fra' Martinus.'

'He won't do anything! He did nothing to get us to see the pope, did he?'

'Not that I could see, but he was very put out when he discovered where we'd been. He's ordered us to be patient and promised that if we are, he'll get us in to see the pope.'

'When?'

'I don't know. I got the impression he's waiting for something.'

'What?'

'I don't know,' Alcuin said as he smiled down at his friend. 'And you are far too tired to even be asking me about things like that. Get some sleep.'

'I feel as if I am in limbo,' Galen murmured. 'Nothing happens here. We never go anywhere.'

'If you behave yourself and eat everything we give you and build up your strength, then I swear we'll go about the city a little more and you can have a proper look around. How does that sound?'

'Like bribery,' Galen said with a slight smile.

The sight of that smile considerably relieved Alcuin. He'd seen Galen depressed before, but not as much as he was now, not in a very long time.

'Fra' Martinus, may I have a word, please?' Alcuin said as he bowed low at the door to the abbot's room that currently also doubled as his place of work.

It was the first time he was seeing it in daylight and the large window behind the abbot filled the room with light, even though it was midwinter.

Despite having a brazier beside him, the man was wrapped in a cloak and a blanket as he moved his finger painstakingly across the paper. For a moment he looked relieved to have this distraction, but then his expression shifted to one of resentment.

'Have you come to see me about Brother Galen?'

'In a manner of speaking, yes.'

'Only in a manner of speaking?' Fra' Martinus said as he indicated for Alcuin to take the chair opposite his desk.

Now that he could see the room in daylight, Alcuin felt as if he'd been transported back in time. All the furniture reminded him of images from manuscripts of what he had imagined were Roman times. He'd not realised how closely those images resembled fact until he saw it himself. The room was larger than he'd guessed from his nighttime visit, with polished wood floors, brick walls and a very high ceiling.

How could man make such grand edifices and then treat them as mere background? How could they not be struck with wonder at the size and decoration of the place? He felt more than ever that he must look like some backwards barbarian.

Alcuin had to remind himself that his namesake, Alcuin of York, had been a great academic. He was an Angle, like Alcuin, who had gone to the court of the great Charlemagne, where he'd been a leading teacher and scholar. And that's what we're good at. These Romans can build mighty edifices out of bricks and stone; we build them with our minds.

'Are you going to answer my question, young man?' Fra' Martinus asked, apparently amused by how Alcuin's eyes widened.

'I beg your pardon. I came because Galen fears something is going to happen to the pope.'

'Almost certainly,' Fra' Martinus said dryly.

That surprised Alcuin. Was this an admission?

'No, you don't understand. Galen fears he is in danger, that he might die.'

'Do you usually give credence to your young friend's premonitions?'

'He doesn't actually have them. I mean, this is a first.'

Alcuin was feeling increasingly stupid to have come, and a sense of futility washed over him.

'He doesn't have premonitions?' Martinus said, and looked intrigued. 'Don't most saints have premonitions and visions almost daily? Surely, even most people you have met have some sort of feelings in their bones or their waters?'

'Not Galen. He doesn't go into flights of fancy, much as he sometimes regrets it.'

'What is there to regret?'

Alcuin watched the abbot warily. He felt the man was fishing as delicately as possible. As it served Alcuin's interests, too, he played along.

'He's never claimed to have a vision. So once, when he thought he had, he was very excited to tell me about it. But when I explained that we'd all seen the same thing, but that he'd had a fever so interpreted it differently, he was disappointed but he didn't stick to it.'

'But not this time?'

'No, I explained that we've all seen things lately because of the contaminated flour, but he persisted. He really believes something bad is going to happen to the pope.'

'Quite likely,' Fra' Martinus said as he leaned back in his chair and crossed his arms.

'So you say, but I don't understand why that doesn't distress you.'

'Do you know anything about the lives of the popes, young man?'

'I have heard tell of the lives of some of the popes who have subsequently become saints.'

'Ah. Do you know about the more modern wrangling of our popes?'

Alcuin shifted uncomfortably on the chair, certain they shouldn't be speaking in such a way about their pontiff.

'Some word of their deeds reaches us in Enga-lond.'

'I discomfort you, but I thought you were of noble birth and aware of the politics of power.'

'I know that our own bishops have that as a concern, but I have tried to distance myself from it.'

'Well, you may as well get used to it, for as the friend of someone who may turn into a saint, you are going to be drawn into that world whether you like it or not.'

'What?'

'Your Bishop Sigburt knew he was onto a powerful pawn with Brother Galen, hence his unseemly haste to come to Rome. And even after his death, the two of you still came, as if swept on by destiny, and you persist in the desire to see the pope.'

'I gave my word to our bishop that I would tell the pope that he was martyred.'

'And you brought Brother Galen.'

'Well... some very strange things happen around him. As the last of those things was bringing me back to life, I can't ignore it. Much as Galen would wish that I could. We have to find somebody to explain it to us.'

'And what if they just say, yes, my son, you are a saint? What do you do then?'

Alcuin blinked at the man.

'I hadn't thought about that.'

'Maybe you should,' Fra' Martinus said and gazed meaningfully at the brazier beside him.

Alcuin got the hint, stood up and fed a couple more logs onto the fire.

'You sound as though you want to keep Galen away from the pope,' he said as he jabbed at the fire with a poker and got the flames jumping.

'I believe he is a good person. I fear what the influence of the pope will be on him. For, Brother Alcuin, the pope's position is one of the most political in the world and because of that, their reigns are seldom long.'

'That's why you think this pope's life is in danger?' Alcuin said. He wished he could remain beside the fire to warm his fingers, but decided it was more important to be able to study the abbot's face, so returned to his seat.

'His life is bound to be at risk. The pope is a very young man, barely twenty-seven. Hence, he is not regarded as fit to rule by many. But as he is the cousin of Emperor Otto, he has got away with it so far. On top of that, until only last year he had opposition in the figure of the Anti-pope John.

'In this instance, the nobles of Rome lost the power struggle and their man was deposed. John is now living in solitude in a Frankish monastery. I suspect, much as he suffered, he will outlive our current pope, for certainly the defeated nobility of Rome will not be content to sit back and forget and forgive. So you see, I live in daily expectation of hearing that the pope has been overthrown or assassinated.'

'So you're trying to protect Galen?' Alcuin said, surprised that this desiccated old man would care to support anyone beside himself.

'I have followed the spread of the contaminated flour across Rome with interest. It seems it was rather a large batch and more than one merchant sold some of this poisonous food. In all cases but one, most of the people who ate bread made from the flour died, except in this monastery, where in every case, the people recovered.'

'Maybe your baker used a lesser quantity of the bad flour in his dough.'

'Ah,' Martinus said, and a smile touched his lips, 'I see why young Galen likes you. You are as level-headed as he is. For you see, others noting this discrepancy are blessing themselves and claiming we've had a little miracle here. It needs only a few whispered hints of all that has been attributed to Brother Galen to get around and we'll have a full-blown case of saint worship on our hands.'

'Which will get around Rome?'

'Like wildfire.'

'And to the pope's ears?'

'Undoubtedly.'

'And that would be a bad idea?'

'With this pope, certainly.'

'We can't wait for another one,' Alcuin cried. 'What if he's just as bad? Do we wait for the next and then the next?'

'I suggest you go alone to the pope. Tell him about your bishop, make no mention of Brother Galen, and then leave as quickly and quietly as you can.'

'I don't know.' This implacable man had filled Alcuin's heart with disquiet. He felt an urgent need to get away, but he knew better than to show it. 'I will consult Galen. We wouldn't be able to leave till the spring anyway, because of the weather over the Alps and because Galen is in no condition to travel yet.'

'You could go by boat, back the way you came. You don't have to go over the mountains.'

'You really want us to leave, don't you?'

'It would be for the best. And having spoken to you properly now, I would urge, in addition, that you deal exclusively with the pope. You are adept at hiding your thoughts; your young friend is not.'

'I know it,' Alcuin said with a nod and accepted his dismissal as Martinus waved him away.

Chapter 13

Carbo was hunched up beside Galen when he woke. He blinked up at the big man and whispered, 'Where's Alcuin?'

'He's getting some sleep. He stays with you all night and as much of the day as possible.'

'Oh,' Galen said. 'Why does he do that?'

'To make sure you'll be alright. I sit with you during the day for a bit so he can work and get some sleep.'

'I must be very ill indeed.'

'You have been,' Carbo said. 'But we are feeling easier about you of late.'

Galen gave a slow nod while trying to further gather his wits and Carbo took it as the cue to get Galen upright and give him some food. He held the feeding bottle to Galen's lips and he sipped the gruel from its spout. He tried to raise his arms to support the small porcelain jar but he didn't have the strength. So he watched the big man tilt the jar and dribble lukewarm gruel into his mouth.

'Thank you, that's enough.'

'You haven't finished it. Alcuin likes you to drink it all.'

'I will in a little while,' Galen said, then leaned back on the pillows and closed his eyes.

Carbo gave a gusty sigh, crossed his hands loosely over each other in his lap and went back to staring out of the hospital door. They were furthest into the room, so the door was far and let in very little of the cold, grey, winter light. He looked so down it cut through Galen's sense of disassociation and pricked his growing guilt.

Galen placed a hand gently on the man's arm. He realised his hands were even thinner and paler than usual, but his fingertips were still stained with ink which flowed into the cracks around his nails, etching them in dark outline.

'You are sad.'

'I'm fine.'

'No,' Galen said, searching Carbo's face. 'You miss your home.'

'It can't be helped.'

'I miss my home, too. But I can't go back, not yet... not for a long time.'

'You'll have to wait until the spring at any rate.'

Galen nodded, watching Carbo's expressions and how slumped and dejected his entire posture was. As filled with wonders as Rome was, it just wasn't home for any of them.

'You should go home now.'

'What, now? When you're still ill. I couldn't do it.'

'Carbo, if someone gave me permission to go now, I wouldn't hesitate. I'd crawl all the way home if I had to.'

'Do you dislike it so much here?'

'It isn't about this place, it's about home. I miss my family and the lands and the abbey. I miss being able to speak my mother tongue, and just being able to feel comfortable and understand everything in word and deed of the people who surround me. I feel very closed in and just... disconnected, so far from home.'

'I feel the same way.'

'Then you should go.'

'What about you? Somebody has to protect you.'

'Alcuin.'

'He is only one man.'

'I know it, and I am a heavy burden to him. I'm trying to be more independent and to look after myself, but if I always have Alcuin and you and all the others who look out for me... well, I am too weak to reject that help.'

'You are doing it now.'

'I'm trying,' Galen said, watching the big man's emotions flicker between hope and anxiety. 'I have known you have been unhappy for a long time and I've only now worked up the courage to send you away.'

'My abbot sent me to look after you.'

'Your role should have ended once we got to Rome.'

'His dream didn't exactly come true.'

'Dreams are a hint of things to come, but you spotted the crucial moment, the time when the similarities to the waking world and the dream made you act, and it saved our lives. I shall always be grateful to you and your fra' for that.'

'Are you sure I should go?'

'I am sure.'

'Will you bless me for my journey?'

Carbo looked uncertain that he should even ask. His life had not always been of the purest and he probably wondered if it was a blasphemy to ask a saint to bless someone as corrupt as him.

Galen tried to reach Carbo's head, but couldn't, so he cupped his hand around the big man's face and said, 'Bless you, Brother Carbo, for you have been a loyal friend. May you find the peace your soul craves.'

Carbo's face lit up. He looked as though a great load had been lifted from his shoulders and he straightened up, apparently filled with renewed vigour.

He grasped Galen's hand, kissed it, and whispered through a throat constricted with emotion, 'Thank you... thank you. I shall never forget you. You may not believe it yet, but you are a saint!'

Then, before tears could overwhelm him, he broke away and hurried off. Despite their rocky beginning, Galen was sorry to see him go, but it was the right thing to do. He offered up a prayer to God that Carbo's journey home would be uneventful. Then he said another one to thank God for his recovery and ask what he should do. He wished God could give him an answer, for his encounter with the pope was still vivid and painful and impossible to understand.

'No,' Carbo said, giving Galen a jolt as he reappeared and hurried back to the bedside. 'I can't go yet.'

Galen was astonished. 'After all you've just said and felt? Your relief to be able to go? Why would you stay?'

'Because I can't leave you yet. As I headed to the dormitory to collect my belongings, I realised that, for now, I have a higher calling. I vowed to my abbot that I would look after you, and I will do so until you get home.'

Carbo's entire demeanour had changed and Galen could tell no argument would shift him.

'It was a moment of weakness,' Carbo said. 'I was tempted to go home, and I will... eventually. For now, I shall remain your faithful hound.'

Galen was touched by this show of devotion but also deeply embarrassed by it.

'I am not worthy of such a sacrifice.'

'It isn't a sacrifice,' Carbo said, grinning broadly as he settled back on his stool, back straight, eyes sparkling. 'It is my new purpose. Home is where you make it and for the time being my home is by your side.'

CHAPTER 14

G alen was in an agony of indecision and rolled about in his bed in equal physical discomfort. Ever since they had arrived in Rome, he'd got no answers to his questions. Months later he was still no clearer on whether or not he was a saint, what it took to be a saint, or how to behave as a saint.

As no miracles had occurred in Rome, he wondered whether being in an abbey protected him from anything else happening. It gave him a measure of reassurance, but fresh doubts frequently overturned it. After all, living in an abbey meant a controlled life, one in which it was also difficult to sin, or, at least, much easier not to sin. He was fully aware that man had difficulty controlling his baser urges and would easily give in to envy, greed or a hundred other little wickednesses that picked away at their souls.

On top of that were his doubts about Brother Bartolo and what he should or should not have done for him, and Sister Marozia and what he should do about her. At least he'd been able to tell her family. Locked away as he was in the abbey, he would most likely never know if or when they would take their revenge. He feared justice was out of the question and that he'd just added fuel to a long family feud.

Those were all problems he had little control over. The biggest question, and the one currently keeping him up at night, was what to do about the pope and his recurring vision of impending doom. Fra' Martinus had made it clear to Alcuin that he was unwilling to communicate with the pope. Alcuin, a far more canny political operator than Galen, had decided the abbot was right.

He'd already apologised to Galen for dragging him all the way to Rome. He'd also said, in his I've made up my mind tone of voice, that when he got an audience with the pope, he would only tell him about the bishop.

Galen groaned in frustration, rolled over and froze. Brother Piero was standing by his bedside.

'Are... are you alright, Brother Galen?'

Galen pushed himself upright and forced a smile to reassure the lad.

'I'm fine, really. I don't know why the infirmarius is insisting I stay in the hospital.'

'I'm sure it won't be for much longer,' Piero said as he settled on the low stool beside the bed. 'I got a special dispensation to visit. Brother Iacopo told me to bring you your Arabic book of numbers. He said it might occupy your mind while you're in bed.'

'I'm grateful for that,' Galen said, taking the proffered work, plus a pen and a stoppered pot of ink.

'He said you were just to read and consider, hence only one pen and not much ink, for annotations and whatnot, nothing more.'

'Very well,' Galen said, blushing to think that the armarius had thought of him at all. 'How are things going with your work?'

'I've nearly finished copying out Boethius. It's been very interesting. Brother Iacopo said my writing is much improved as well and that my copy will go into the abbey library.'

'Excellent news,' Galen said, swelling with pride that his protégé was doing so well. Then a thought struck him. 'Piero... do you know the Theophylacti?'

Piero looked taken aback but said, 'I know of them, of course, and I know where they live.'

'Do you think... could you get a message to them for me?' Galen asked and instantly regretted it. 'No, don't worry. It isn't something I should ask of you.'

It wasn't something he should do at all. The fra' and Alcuin would both be annoyed.

'Why would you have anything to say to them?' Piero asked. 'Have you ever even met one of them?'

Galen shook his head, not in denial but trying to drive the temptation away. Then he clenched his fists and decided. He would accept the consequences later, but this was a decision he had to make.

'Actually... could you get a message to them?'

'Why?'

'The less you know, the better. I already feel guilty for dragging you into this.'

Piero gazed down at him with such a worried expression it nearly made Galen back out again.

Then Piero said, 'If that is what you wish, I will do it.'

'So you can!'

Piero nodded and Galen clasped his hand in gratitude.

'Just give me a moment to craft my letter.'

He hunted through Hatim's manuscript, found a quarter page that he could cut out and wrote his short note.

Lady Chedira, if you still feel you owe me a favour, then I would like to take you up on it.

CHAPTER 15

Galen's anxiety mounted as he waited for a reply from the Theophylacti. The infirmarius also remained constant in his denial to release Galen back into the abbey. So he hadn't seen Piero and even Alcuin could only come by to visit twice a day. Carbo was his most frequent visitor, but even he'd been told to go back to work in the kitchen.

Galen felt guilty about going behind Alcuin's back and so their conversations felt constrained. Alcuin, thankfully, put it down to Galen not being fully recovered. All the same, despite his guilt, Galen was always happy to see his friend.

He'd just finished his dinner, eaten in bed, with the blanket pulled up to under his arms because it was getting colder and colder as winter progressed, when Alcuin arrived.

'I'm glad to see you are at least eating well,' Alcuin said, taking in the empty bowl.

'And as a patient, I get given meat with every meal, so I feel like I'm being spoiled.'

'It's necessary to rebuild your strength,' Alcuin said as he settled on the bed opposite. He pulled a small, tightly folded note out of his pocket and handed it to Galen. 'Your student asked me to give you this.'

Galen's breath froze in his chest. Piero had given the note to Alcuin! He knew he wouldn't read something private, but he was almost overwhelmed by guilt to have his friend deliver something he'd wanted to keep from him.

'Thank you,' Galen said and couldn't prevent his hand from shaking as he took the note.

'Are you alright?' Alcuin asked, so filled with concern that Galen's guilt doubled. 'Are you running a fever? Your face has just gone red!'

Alcuin's concern felt like the cuts of a whip to Galen's conscience.

'Oh, Alcuin, I'm so sorry!'

'Sorry about what? What could you possibly have done?'

'I've been deceiving you.'

'You have? No, how could that be? You're incapable of deceiving anyone.'

'I... I have been trying to arrange a meeting with the pope.'

Galen's voice sank to a whisper and his gaze fixed on the bed because he couldn't face seeing Alcuin's disappointment in him.

'You've been trying to see the pope? How...' Alcuin paused and Galen didn't dare to look up to find out why. 'Is this note something to do with it?'

Galen nodded.

'I asked Piero to use his connections, and... you remember, Lady Chedira said she owed me a favour, so...'

'Well, you'd best look at the note then,' Alcuin said, his voice flat.

Galen gave him a guilty peek to find the mask had come down and Alcuin was giving nothing away, although he'd crossed his arms, which wasn't a good sign. Galen, despite his regret, felt a little better that at least Alcuin knew now. Although, he feared he was in for a fierce battle with his friend and he had his doubts about winning it.

The note was as short as his own had been.

This Sunday, noon, the same church as before.

Galen held the note out to Alcuin who took it in at a glance.

'To meet the pope?'

'He wouldn't go to that church. I assume it's explaining what can be done, or maybe agree on how a meeting is arranged.'

'Galen, you stubborn little fool,' Alcuin said, and now he looked angry.

'I'm sorry,' Galen said, hanging his head, 'but I can't explain the fear I feel. The vision repeats itself endlessly in my dreams and during my waking hours. I feel driven to do this.'

'But I've already told you, we all ate poisonous bread. You know what that's like, for it's common enough. Everyone suffered from hallucinations.'

'The thing is... the thing is, Alcuin... I didn't eat any bread that day.'

'You didn't?' Alcuin said, sitting back with a jerk.

'What with the earth shaking and the long walk, I didn't feel up to eating much. So I just ate some of the cheese.'

'But you collapsed right after seeing the pope, and you threw up blood.'

'I know, and the feeling that went along with it, the foreboding, was even more intense.'

Alcuin sighed.

'Of course, that would weigh on you. I suppose knowing that every pope's life is always at risk is no reassurance.'

'Not with such strange premonitions.'

'They do seem very doom-laden. I'm sorry, Galen, I should have listened to you properly, not ridden roughshod over you as always.'

'I should have spoken up sooner too,' Galen said, feeling bad that he'd upset Alcuin.

'You tried, but I didn't listen. And around here, everything is trickier. If you meet that woman again, the abbot will most likely be furious.'

'I know, but at the same time I don't want to tell him lest he bar me from going.'

Galen's stomach gave a nervous flutter as he, Alcuin and Carbo set off along the lane that led from the abbey to the church of Saints Cosmo and Damiano. Carbo had insisted that he take much of Galen's weight as he walked, which was necessary as Galen hadn't quite recovered from his illness. Both of Galen's companions looked relaxed as they wended their slow way through the pedestrians.

Carbo made most of them go around the monks, rather than the other way, which Alcuin seemed to approve of. It was a considerable relief that Alcuin now knew everything and wasn't angry.

'Don't be a fool, of course I have to go,' Alcuin had said when Galen suggested going alone. 'You'll never make it on your own. Besides, our order requires that monks always go out in pairs. And we'll take Carbo along to help with the walk and in case we need defending.'

Galen had nodded guilty agreement. This was another rule he'd broken more than once. But now he was glad he wouldn't have to sneak out on his own.

'Carbo won't be happy when he hears what we're up to.'

Alcuin shrugged in an exaggerated way that made him look like a Roman. It seemed he was assimilating.

'Carbo will do whatever you want. Now more than ever.'

'I wish he wouldn't,' Galen said, because Carbo's veneration made him uncomfortable.

He also worried what the other monks might make of such open adoration.

'There's no stopping him,' Alcuin said, 'although I've tried. But today he will be useful. I've also cleared our trip with both the fra' and the infirmarius. I've told everyone that we want to pray to Cosmo and Damiano for healing.'

Galen nodded and said, 'I was going to do that anyway.'

Now, as Galen watched, Alcuin pulled his cloak about himself as a sharp wind whistled between the buildings, blowing a few remaining crispy dark leaves with it. The crowds this morning were also more subdued, as if the grey clouds and cold weather sapped the will to speak. Even the hawkers sounded muffled.

They passed a baker, his shop front wide open, the loaves cooling on the stone bench at the entrance while flames roared in his oven at the back, basking everyone who passed in warmth. More than one pedestrian paused there, lifting their hands to warm their fingers before hurrying on. The smell, too, was delicious and, nervous as Galen felt, even he was tempted. Not that they had money for treats, and the bakery of the abbey was also excellent, so he couldn't complain.

On they walked, Alcuin keeping a wary eye out for any potential ambush.

'Thank goodness Carbo is still with us,' he muttered, glancing up at the big man.

'It's a good thing he is. Although I feel guilty about dragging you into this,' Galen said, looking up at Carbo.

'No need to feel bad. It's what I'm here for,' Carbo said and waved his stout staff about for emphasis, which got a man carrying a heavy load of logs to hastily step out of their way.

'All the same.'

It felt to Galen like he was taking too much and giving back too little. But now wasn't the time to be distracted. The lane they were on petered out, the houses growing smaller and less impressive until they arrived at the field of ruins. The ground here was soggy after a week of persistent rain and the band of monks squelched down a muddy path, past tall Roman marble columns to the severe plain façade of the basilica.

Lady Chedira had brought even more guards today and there were eight armed men at the door, all on high alert.

'Well, that's not intimidating at all,' Alcuin murmured.

Galen tried for a smile that probably looked more like a grimace as fear mingled with pain and exhaustion. He wondered whether they should say anything to the men, perhaps explain who they were and whom they'd come to see. But Alcuin just sailed past them and Carbo did the same, although Galen felt the big man's muscles tense. Since he was holding Galen's arm, he had no choice but to go, too. In the event, the men did nothing but look them up and down as they stepped into the dark beyond.

Lady Chedira was standing in the middle of the church, wrapped in a voluminous deep red cape, rubbing her hands together thoughtfully.

'My lady,' Galen said, executing a bow at the same time as Alcuin and Carbo.

'Who are they?'

'My friends, Brothers Alcuin and Carbo; they were here last time as well.'

Lady Chedira gave Alcuin and Carbo a thoughtful look and said, 'Yes, perhaps I remember them.'

It surprised Galen that she'd paid so little attention to his companions, but supposed it was understandable since their meeting was supposed to be a secret and she'd also received shocking news.

'So now you want to meet the pope, is that it?' Lady Chedira said.

Galen inclined his head, trying to look as calm as the lady did and said, 'Is that something you can arrange?'

'As I told you before, it's possible, but not advisable.'

Galen avoided looking at Alcuin, for he'd said the same thing, as had everybody else.

'I know, but—'

A shout from outside combined with the clash of weapons froze the words on his lips as Carbo put his staff in front of Galen like a shield.

'What?' Alcuin muttered and stepped across Galen to hide him.

Both doors were flung open and a dozen soldiers, armed with spears, trooped in. Galen tried to move out from behind Alcuin's protection, but his legs were too shaky and Carbo's grip on his arm too firm.

Pope Gregory stepped inside and stalked down the aisle of soldiers, his white and gold cape flapping behind him, making him look even bigger.

Dizziness overwhelmed Galen, and it wasn't just the shock of seeing this terrifying man. The pope's face had turned as white as bone and his eyes were so sunken that Galen felt like he was staring into the sockets of a skeleton.

'Your Holiness,' Alcuin said and dropped to his knees, dragging Carbo and Galen down with him.

Galen wanted to resist. His whole body was telling him this man wasn't worthy of respect, but he was pulled down and his knees hit the marble floor with a solid crack. Lady Chedira had also lowered herself to her knees, her fierce eyes on the door, clearly wondering what had happened to her guards, for all was silent outside.

'So, this is where your allegiance lies,' the pope said. His voice was smooth and reassuring, like one delivering a sermon, even while his words were menacing.

Galen tried to get up, struggling against Carbo's grip that was keeping him down.

'Your Holiness,' Galen said, his words soft and shaky, 'I have a warning for you.'

'Threats... right away?' the pope said, tilting his head and gazing down at Galen with his flat, lifeless, grey eyes as if Galen was a mote of dust.

'Not a threat, a warning,' Galen said desperately, his spit drying up in his mouth. 'I see... such a terrible fate. Please, Your Holiness, exercise the greatest of care.'

'That's rich coming from you,' the pope said, and his holy-sounding voice took on a sharper edge. 'You who have sided with the Theophylacti.'

'All he did was tell me what happened to my cousin,' Lady Chedira said as she rose to her feet. 'Will you deny that your hands are red with Marozia's blood and the blood of her followers?'

'You know even better than I what she was planning. What your entire accursed family is planning. Well, I won't let it happen,' the pope said, and his voice boomed across the church and echoed around them.

'Were you really responsible for that massacre?' Galen whispered as the echoes of the pope's voice faded.

'I will do what it takes to protect the papacy,' Gregory said. 'But I am not unreasonable. I have not made a move against you monks even after my servant Bartolo told me about you.'

'He told you?' Galen asked, and he felt even more disappointed in the man.

'Shortly before he died,' the pope said and closed the distance between himself and Galen. 'Which is why I've had my people watching you ever since.' He grabbed Galen's chin and tilted his head this way and that, examining his face. 'He said you might be a saint,' the pope whispered in Galen's ear.

It felt like his face was on fire. Bile flooded his mouth and Galen shoved both hands against the pope's chest and pushed away with all his strength. He flew backwards, toppled over and lay stunned. He felt as drained as when the king's leech had drawn his blood.

The pope took another step towards him, but this time Alcuin intervened.

'Please, Your Holiness, Brother Galen merely wanted to warn you that your life is in danger. Despite all of us telling him not to, he made this great effort to come. Please, now that you have heard what he has to say, let us return to the abbey and we will never trouble you again.'

It seemed to take a great deal of effort for the pope to drag his eyes away from Galen and onto Alcuin.

'Let them go,' Lady Chedira said, 'for if you try to harm them, my house will provide them with protection.'

'Do you think your handful of guards is a match for my men?' the pope said, and his voice dripped disdain.

'They will fight and die for me and mine. But, let me ask you, how many more of my family will you kill to keep your secret? And how well can you keep a secret if you keep committing wholesale massacres?'

'Please, Your Holiness,' Galen whispered, while Carbo helped him back onto his knees. 'Save yourself before it's too late. Repent, do penance and make your peace with God.'

'God has never forsaken me,' the pope roared. 'Look at the station to which I have been elevated. Do you, puny saint, think you even approach my level?'

'Of course not,' Galen said, struggling against the overwhelming sense of dread to raise his head and look at the man.

'No,' Gregory said, but the fight went out of him at Galen's capitulation and he turned back to Alcuin. 'I will hold you to your word. If you step out of the abbey again, it will be the last thing you ever do.'

'Thank you, Your Holiness,' Alcuin said, giving a deep bow.

'And you,' the pope said, pointing a finger at Lady Chedira, 'I have my eye on you as well. One wrong move and I will erase every single member of the Theophylacti without a moment of remorse. Your poison has spread far enough.'

The lady bowed her head but looked unimpressed. Galen doubted the pope saw it, for he turned on his heels and left, his guards closing about him.

'Galen!' Alcuin said, and hurried to his side the moment they were alone again. 'Are you alright?'

'I feel as weak as a newborn,' Galen said softly.

'I'm not surprised, that was terrifying,' Alcuin said and wiped the back of his hand across his forehead which was beaded with sweat. 'But at least you did what you needed to do.'

'Without my help,' Lady Chedira said and sat down on a wooden bench with a relieved sigh. 'All in all, that went better than I feared at the start. I also got the irrefutable confirmation that it was the pope who ordered Marozia's death. So it seems I owe you an even greater favour now.'

'I have no need of favours,' Galen said, trying to gather his thoughts while Carbo helped him up and to the bench opposite Lady Chedira. 'But I still fear for the pope. He looked ghastly.'

'Ghastly? He looked no different from how he always looks, although he is prone to flamboyance. I didn't think his cape was entirely tasteful.'

'No, not his clothes, his face. It was so pale and skeletal that it was terrifying,' Galen said and wondered why Alcuin and Lady Chedira looked surprised by his words.

'He looked perfectly normal and healthy to me,' Alcuin said.

'Me too,' Lady Chedira said.

'And me,' Carbo said.

'Really?' Galen asked, because there was no way what he had seen was normal. 'And his aura of malevolence?'

'Just pomposity,' Lady Chedira said.

'And the intimidation one feels around people of power,' Alcuin said.

'No,' Galen murmured.

That hadn't been it, nor had it been a hallucination. So was it a vision? He was too shaken to think about that at the moment so just gave a nod to Carbo's questioning look. He was ready to go.

'So you are a saint, too?' Lady Chedira said once Galen was up and had regained his breath.

'Ah,' Galen said, sharing a look with Alcuin. 'That isn't confirmed yet.'

'Did you speak to Marozia about it?'

'I did.'

'What did she say?'

'That I had to make my own decision and not allow others to pull me this way and that based on their needs and desires.'

'That is exactly what she would say,' Lady Chedira said. 'Now, you look very pale, and I believe it is time to get you home. I will have a few of my guards accompany you to make sure you aren't ambushed along the way.'

Galen shuddered, wondering whether she meant the pope, or just a mugger.

'Thank you.'

Lady Chedira nodded and said, 'Take the pope's words to heart. Remain in the abbey if you value your life.'

CHAPTER 16

Alcuin was shaken by the meeting with the pope and couldn't concentrate all the way through the chapter house meeting. It didn't help that the order of business today was the repair of the visitors' hall roof. It had apparently sprung several leaks owing to the unusually heavy winter rain. It was important, of course, but nothing to do with Alcuin.

So his mind drifted to thinking about Galen. Ever since Galen had saved his life, he'd tried to ignore the fact that Galen was a saint. It was a fact he was growing to accept by the day.

It made him regret that he'd treated his friend's concerns over the matter so lightly until it had impacted on him directly. Until now, like Galen, he'd pushed all thoughts about sainthood to the back of his mind and tried to focus on day-to-day life. But now there was this thing, this urgent need, that had driven his painfully shy friend to meet with a terrifying man.

There, he'd seen the world differently. A pope that looked like a skeleton, being warned that he was approaching death. This was entirely unlike Galen. Alcuin couldn't help but feel it had to be God working through him.

This had to be faced, not simply pushed aside. Had they all been wrong to do so until now? To bumble along without giving it the consideration that things of such moment required? Alcuin thought so, and was tempted to lay the blame on Galen for ignoring it.

Then again, Galen worried away at the question all the time and was surely addressing it in his prayers every day. So, no, it wasn't his fault. But what a great burden to bear. Alcuin had to do more to help.

He realised the chapter house was now nearly empty as the last few monks vanished into the cloister. Now there was only him and, to his dismay, the abbot. He had his hands folded over the knob of his walking stick and his head resting on top of that, eyeing Alcuin unblinkingly. As the abbot was noticed, he straightened up and crooked his finger, calling Alcuin closer.

'You want a word, Fra' Martinus?' Alcuin said as he made his way over and knelt at the old man's feet.

'My porter tells me you and Brothers Galen and Carbo went out yesterday.'

Alcuin flushed as his conscience pricked at him.

'We did.'

'Might I ask where?'

The question was asked blandly, with no trace of irritation, but Alcuin knew he was in danger of causing offence.

'We went to the Basilica of Saints Cosmo and Damiano to pray for Galen's recovery.'

Alcuin prayed he wouldn't be pushed further while wondering whether he should confess all. They could no longer leave the abbey if they wanted to be safe, and that might become an issue later.

'And?'

'We wanted to get some fresh air.'

'So much fresh air in fact that you returned accompanied by an armed guard?'

'Ah!'

Alcuin sighed. He could lie, but there was no point.

'Galen — We knew it was unlikely, but we hoped we might arrange a way to speak to the pope.'

'It was Brother Galen's idea?'

'No,' Alcuin said, and then his shoulders slumped. 'Yes.'

'Your wish to protect your friend is laudable, but you gave yourself away with your first word,' Fra' Martinus's said. 'The tyranny of the weak, you see? He had you doing exactly what he wanted.'

The abbot's voice was tinged with sarcasm. That angered Alcuin but he couldn't do a thing about it and the man wasn't entirely wrong.

'Galen was very worried. He doesn't normally go into heights of angst, so I knew it wasn't normal.'

'He could have died in the street,' Fra' Martinus said. 'Instead, he may well die in the infirmary. But rest assured that if he survives, I will get him to see the pope if he is so determined. In the meantime, he will have to work on gaining some saintly patience and you focus on some worldly patience.'

'Ah...' Alcuin said, aware that now he would have to explain all. 'As it happens, we did see the pope.'

'You did?' Fra' Martinus said. 'Well, I suppose that explains the armed guards.'

Deceptions were always so difficult to disentangle, Alcuin thought with a sigh.

'I will have to explain everything. It's rather complicated.'

Alcuin told the abbot all about their meeting with the pope, because he hoped the abbot might have an insight into everything.

But in the end all the abbot said was, 'Dear Lord! Well, at least you now know where you stand with the pope. I will warn Brother Donato to be especially careful as to whom he allows in from now on.'

'Thank you,' Alcuin said.

He was relieved that the fra' was still willing to protect them. If he'd decided to eject them from the abbey, they'd have been in grave danger.

Galen felt impossibly weak after his confrontation with the pope. It was as if the man had sucked his life essence out of him. That thought made him shudder. He played the events of the day over and over in his mind, trying to decide what he made of it. The fact that the pope had looked different to him was what puzzled him the most.

So he rolled onto his side and surveyed the hospital. Alcuin had brought him back here because he was now more determined than ever that Galen should rest and recover fully before returning to the scriptorium. Over the long time that he'd been its occupant, it had grown fuller and then emptier and then fuller again as the days passed and as patients turned up and left. Now there were only five men occupying beds at the other end of the hall.

Galen felt lonely. Carbo and Alcuin had offered to keep him company, but Galen had insisted they go back to work and only visit a couple of times a day. He regretted it and especially missed Alcuin's company. But he couldn't keep Alcuin tied to him, willing as he appeared to do it. Now, though, he felt deserted, and a grey depression sucked the colour out of his life.

Alcuin had relayed his entire conversation with the abbot that morning in a low-voiced whisper. It had depressed Galen, although he wasn't sure why. He supposed it was because neither man had given him any helpful answers. Deep down he'd hoped for someone who lived up to the reputation of the pope for wisdom and goodness. Even deeper down, barely acknowledged, he'd hoped for one who embodied the title of papa. Someone who could honestly and kindly guide him out of his dilemma.

But the more he considered it, the more he realised he was the only one who could solve his predicament. He had to find his own solution. That filled him with more doubt. How was he supposed to come to a conclusion when all his prayers for guidance remained unanswered?

Maybe the answer was for him to do what so many saints before him had done. Maybe he had to go away from it all and become a hermit. That thought made the depression smother him.

Much as he feared people and found himself uncomfortable in their presence, he didn't want to be alone. He wanted company and to be surrounded by a few good friends and family. That thought brought up images of his mother and sisters and even his father, and tears welled unbidden to his eyes.

'Galen, are you alright?' Alcuin said as he dropped to his haunches beside his friend.

Galen hastily rubbed away the tears with his palm and said, 'I'm fine.'

'It doesn't seem like it. Lately you've been very down.'

'I miss home and my family. I'm exhausted, both physically and mentally.'

Alcuin nodded and continued to watch Galen closely.

'You carry a heavy burden and I am only now starting to understand it. I'm sorry it's taken me so long.'

Galen waved away the apology. He couldn't face yet another conversation about what he might or might not be.

'Do you miss your family, Alcuin? You never say.'

Alcuin shrugged and then seemed to decide that more was needed.

'The family bond is supposed to be strong. We're meant to stand by each other. But, maybe because I was sent away to the monastery so young, I'm not as close to my family as I should be. I'm accustomed to being away from them.'

Galen sighed and Alcuin gave his shoulder a reassuring pat, then took a deep breath and said, 'I wasn't going to say anything about it, but the two of us are brothers, you know?'

'We're in the same order,' Galen murmured. 'We're all brothers.'

'More than that. I can't say this to anyone else, but I can say it to you. We're related because no matter how illicit our affair, Emma's child is my child. That links the two of us in blood.'

'Oh!' Galen said, his eyes widening in surprise.

Alcuin waited, and Galen knew why. To be reminded that his sister had dishonoured her family by producing an illegitimate child was enough to sever any friendship. But Galen had no intention of doing that.

'You're right!' he said, perceiving this wonder. 'We are family!'

'I'm glad you think so. Feuds have sprung up over less.'

'Oh no, not between you and me, Alcuin.'

'That was what I hoped. Phew! It was still a risk coming out and saying it, though. You have no idea how long this truth has been burning away in my mind.'

'I'm glad you told me. I don't know why I didn't work it out myself.'

'You've had more important things on your mind.'

'One of which is that I keep you tied to me when I have no right.'

'Well, we're family, so we stick together,' Alcuin said with a laugh. 'You'll never be able to get rid of me, you know, not now. Not when you are the only other person to know about me, Emma, and the baby.'

'You don't know that the child was born safely, Alcuin,' Galen said, suddenly worried. 'You should be wary lest you are devastated by bad news later.'

'Not me. Not with you for her brother. I know deep in my heart that they are both alright.'

'There is no proof.'

'There is just you. I choose to believe that you will keep them and the rest of your family safe.'

Galen was stunned by the blind belief from Alcuin but bit back his first thought that if he was protecting his family, Willnoth wouldn't have died. He couldn't bring himself to hurt Alcuin and, really, they were going to be here for a long time. Who knew if they'd ever get back home, so he wouldn't throw a damper on his friend's spirits.

Alcuin laughed and said, 'Thank you for not trying to disabuse me. I saw your doubts clearly on your face, but no matter what you said to me, you wouldn't be able to sway me on this.'

'Then I won't try.'

'Good, I—' Alcuin stopped and tilted his head to listen.

'Running,' Galen said of the unfamiliar commotion outside. 'Why?'

'I don't know, and I don't like it.'

'There's more than one,' Galen said as disquiet crept up on him. 'I didn't feel an earthquake,' he added, for that was all he could think of that would make monks run. It was against the rules, after all.

'You stay here. I'll find out what's happened.'

Galen nodded and watched as Alcuin made stealthily outside. Then Galen took a deep breath and pushed himself upright. He'd done enough wallowing. He had to get better now and be up for walking so that they could go home, and for now, so that they could flee if necessary.

When Alcuin got back, Galen was standing beside his bed, swaying gently and looking out of focus.

'What on earth are you doing?'

'Getting ready in case we had to leave in a hurry.'

'No such chance,' Alcuin said as he took Galen by the elbow and sat him back down on his bed.

'So what's going on?'

'The pope has died.'

'Oh!'

'It was what you feared, wasn't it?'

'My premonition came true?' Galen whispered. 'And right after we saw him!'

'No, remember that Fra' Martinus said this was inevitable. Anyone living in the city could predict such an outcome.'

'How did he die? Was he murdered?' Galen asked as a sick feeling welled up.

After all he had done, Pope Gregory had still died.

'They found him dead in his bed, but apparently without a mark on him. Considering he was only twenty-seven, I fear it looks like he was poisoned. Although one of the brothers thinks the powers that be may want to play that down. Nobody wants a return to war over the next pope.'

'What of us? What do we do?'

Alcuin sat down beside him and said softly, so that the other patients couldn't overhear them, 'That all depends. I don't suppose this new pope will care much about the business of his predecessor, so he probably won't be interested in why Bishop Sigburt never arrived. And after what Fra' Martinus told me, I'm not sure you should speak to any pope, no matter how good they are. But we no longer have the pope's threat hanging over us, either. Maybe we should just wait for the spring and then slip off.'

'In the meantime, I'll work on getting back into a shape where I can walk all day,' Galen said, happy that they had a resolution of sorts. 'I'm going to have to do that if we're to go over the mountains.'

Alcuin took a deep breath and said, 'We could always go by boat. I've been told you can nearly do the entire journey by river and sea.'

Galen smiled at the depth of Alcuin's friendship and shook his head.

'No, we'll walk. I feel like I can do it easily enough and not suffer nearly as much as you suffer on a boat. Besides, there are sure to be monasteries along the route.'

'Good, then we have a plan,' Alcuin said with a wide, relieved grin. 'I'm looking forward to leaving already.'

CHAPTER 17

It was February before Galen was allowed out of the infirmary and back to the scriptorium. He'd planned to just slip inside without creating a fuss, but in that, Piero foiled him.

'Brother Galen!' he said as Galen was heading for his desk. 'You're back!'

He looked so pleased it embarrassed Galen.

'Good lord, look at that,' Brother Luca said. 'How is it possible for you to turn pink with pleasure to return to our daily grind? If I were you, Brother, I'd have stayed in the infirmary and slept to my heart's content.'

'Of course you would,' Brother Feo said as he wiped at his watering eye with a handkerchief. 'But we all know Brother Galen is a much harder worker than you. He even finished translating that Arabic text while he was still in the infirmary.'

'And I've been making a copy for our library,' Brother Bosso said. 'It's very well translated. My head hurts just to think about arithmetic but even I can understand this different numbering system and it does appear to be easier to use.'

Galen blinked at everyone, surprised that he was just included, as if he'd always been a part of them.

'I... thought it was much easier too,' he murmured as he settled behind his desk.

'Here's something that requires a meticulous hand,' Brother Iacopo said as he put a codex down before Galen. 'An account of Pope Gregory's life, as dictated by Cardinal Gui. Now we need it to be made into a codex.'

'P-Pope Gregory's life?' Galen said, astonished that they had given him this task.

It almost felt like a penance ordained by God for his failure to save the pope. Alcuin, who'd been grinning a welcome at Galen, immediately jumped up to come and look at the dictated notes.

'The final codex will be given as a gift to the emperor with a suitably grand cover of ivory and gold,' Brother Iacopo said. 'It is hoped that may placate him and prevent him from going on a witch hunt.'

'But... why me?'

'Because you have the neatest handwriting,' Brother Iacopo said. 'There is no deeper meaning than that.'

'But who is Cardinal Gui?' Brother Bosso asked. 'And why has he written this biography in such haste?'

'I would say to curry favour with the emperor.'

'Do you think he wants to be the next pope?'

'I doubt that. He might not be well known amongst the people, but the cardinal is a canny political operator. He wields his power behind the scenes. Which is probably why he has survived at the Lateran Palace for over twenty-five years, during which time we have gone through six popes, official and otherwise.'

'Pope Gregory didn't even make it to three years,' Luca said with a gigantic yawn. 'Which was probably why the funeral was so unimpressive.'

'Was it?' Galen asked before he could stop himself.

'It was full of pomp at the Lateran,' Brother Iacopo said.

He would know. Alcuin had already told Galen that a delegation of the abbey's senior men had attended the funeral.

'But it seems the citizens of Rome weren't overly enamoured of him,' Brother Iacopo said. 'People came out to line the streets, but it had a perfunctory feel to it, like they were just curious onlookers.'

'It must be difficult getting worked up when there are so many great people in a place,' Galen said. 'So many kings, emperors, bishops and even the pope.'

'It makes them an arrogant lot,' Alcuin whispered in Galen's ear, 'always looking down their noses at us.'

Galen smiled and said, 'They mostly have to look up to look at you.'

'You know what I mean.'

'And we still don't have a new pope,' Brother Feo said, 'which always leads to unrest. The sooner they install a new pope, the better.'

'Do we have any idea who it might be?' Brother Bosso asked.

'There are as many rumours and guesses as there are nobles in Rome,' Brother Iacopo said, 'and we have wasted enough time in useless speculation. So get back to work.'

'Ah, Brother,' Alcuin said, waving an arm in the air as he made his way back to his desk, 'I have two requests. The first is to illustrate the codex on Gregory.'

'I will consider it.'

'The second is that Galen and I be allowed to take a few afternoons off. The infirmarius has said that Galen must do more walking.'

Brother Iacopo gave an exasperated sigh but nodded.

'I have also been informed about that, so I will allow it. And aside from those two orders, I would also like Brother Galen to teach Brothers Piero and Bosso to read Arabic. It would be useful for the future of our abbey to be able to translate from that script.'

'Oh,' Galen said and felt his face grow warm with pride and embarrassment. He felt like he was being treated far too well in this scriptorium, and he wasn't sure he deserved it. But his shyness also prevented him from refusing. He'd really enjoyed being able to help Piero find his feet in the scriptorium and was eager to share more of what he'd learned as well.

CHAPTER 18

True to his word, the very next day, Alcuin led Galen through the streets of Rome, this time heading north.

'No Carbo today? Galen said.

'I decided we wouldn't need him. We aren't going far.'

Galen wasn't surprised to see a slight flush tinge Alcuin's cheeks, and not for the first time when talking about Carbo.

'Do you dislike him?'

'Why would you ask that?' Alcuin said, threading his way between the people crowded on the narrow pavements, shopping and arguing.

'It has seemed to me, even when you are pleased with what he's done, that you don't altogether like him. I know he is slow and rambles on sometimes, but he means well.'

'Ah,' Alcuin said and stopped.

He pulled himself and Galen out of the stream of people and leaned against the shop wall as he ran his hand ruefully through his hair. 'It isn't his lumbering nature, nor his simplicity that annoys me. Well, it's not the main thing, anyway.'

'What then?' Galen asked, astonished that Alcuin, who was so good at hiding his feelings, was looking embarrassed.

'Would you believe I... I'm sometimes jealous of him?' he said in a rush.

'Jealous? You? With your talents and fine looks? What on earth does he have that is better than you?'

Alcuin laughed, blushing even deeper and said, 'I knew you wouldn't get it. I'm envious of how he sometimes takes you away from me.'

Galen blinked at Alcuin, completely unable to understand.

'It's not because you're a saint,' Alcuin said, patting Galen's back. 'It's just because I was your friend first and, God help me, sometimes I don't want it to change. Which I know is selfish and I am working to be a better man and merely be glad for you when you make other friends. I'm not half as bothered by Brother Piero, for example.'

Galen felt his own face grow warm and then he laughed because the situation was so ridiculous and Alcuin looked so shamefaced.

'I'm sorry, I shouldn't have laughed, but you have no need to fear. You will always be my friend, my boon companion and my family, no matter how many hundreds of people come after. I will forever be grateful for that.'

The laugh broke Alcuin's squirming shame and he joined in, saying, 'So let's just enjoy ourselves today, huh? Just you and me, free from the pope's threat to kill us if we left.'

Galen shuddered to be reminded of that and said, 'I'm still not sure what to make of the vision.'

'I've been thinking about that and I wonder... This may sound strange, but you said you were repulsed by the pope. You were also prevented from getting to him when you threw up and collapsed.'

'That's true.'

'What if...' Alcuin said, and stepped further out onto the pavement, which caused a man carrying a large sack of flour to bump into him and start cursing. Alcuin ignored him, while Galen tried to step further back to clear the way. 'What if God was trying to keep you away from him?'

'Keep me away?' Galen said, trying to listen with an open mind, but it sounded ridiculous.

'Listen,' Alcuin said, setting off again, for he couldn't cause too much of a blockage. 'One saint already warned that man, Gregory, to mend his ways. Then you came along and told him much the same, and what did he do? Threatened you with death if you ever said a word.'

'He didn't feel like a particularly godly man,' Galen said, 'but I don't understand why God would try to keep me away from him. Especially since we were having such difficulty convincing anyone that we should see him.'

'But that's the point. Everything stood in your way,' Alcuin said, scratching his head. 'Well, never mind, I suppose it's yet another mystery.'

'One of many,' Galen said with a laugh as he crossed the road, keeping close to Alcuin to ensure a trundling cart or pack horse didn't separate them.

They carried on for only a dozen more paces until they came to a square filled with merchants and craftsmen. At the far end of the space sat a huge, squat building, the rear of which was circular, but the front lined with three rows of pillars.

'Another place built by the Ancient Romans,' Alcuin said. 'Brother Feo recommended it. They called it the Pantheon and it was apparently filled with the idols of the Roman gods. Now it is the Church of Saint Mary of the Martyrs.'

'It's huge, and all in one piece. Not many of the Roman buildings are in such good condition. Imagine, Alcuin,' Galen said with an excited shudder, 'that building has been standing for a thousand years. It has been on Earth for as long as Jesus has been back in heaven.'

'That's quite a thought,' Alcuin said. 'I doubt I've ever seen anything to equal its age.'

Galen nodded, his eyes fixed on the building, barely taking in all the people about him. Alcuin helped Galen into the building and the two of them stopped on the threshold.

'It's incredible!' Galen said as his eyes swept upwards, following the pattern of the stone that set one square into another and another and formed into a ring of squares that climbed in circles to form a mighty dome pierced at its apex with a circular void which, aside from the door, was all that brought in light. It was sufficient. The space was light enough to see that the walls below the dome were covered in an intricate pattern of inset pillars.

'Look at the colours,' Alcuin breathed. 'Who could have believed that stone could come in such a variety of shades? See how they laid them into a pattern, Galen!'

'It is very beautiful.'

'And it was a long walk and you're tired. Come, let's find a place to sit if we can amongst this multitude of pilgrims.'

As he spoke, he pointed to a gap that Galen could occupy and still take in the spectacular view. Galen slid his back down the wall till he was sitting on the floor, his knees drawn up, and looked about in amazement. He felt lightheaded from the exercise and relieved to be sitting, but he wouldn't have missed seeing this Pantheon for the world.

'Are you alright?' Alcuin said.

'I'm fine.'

'But you're in pain.'

'That doesn't go away,' Galen said with a slight, embarrassed smile.

'Is it a bit better, though?'

'Oh yes, Hatim's surgery has worked wonders. I haven't bled since we escaped his uncle's palace, even when Carbo landed on top of me.'

'That is certainly a good sign. I just don't understand why the pain doesn't go away if Hatim solved the problem of the bleeding.'

'I don't know for certain,' Galen said, 'but I think... I think something deeper inside was broken. It moves about when I walk... grinding... getting more painful as the day passes.'

Alcuin shuddered, which made Galen feel even more grateful for his friendship.

'I'll make sure you don't have to walk too far in a day.'

'I am better with that, too. Once I couldn't even contemplate walking for a whole day.'

'Perhaps everything that happens then is for a reason. Perhaps we had to fall into Moorish hands so that you could be healed, if only partially.'

Galen leaned his head back against the wall, looking up at the light flooding in above.

'Surely it would have been easier just to heal me than to have to engineer such an intricate web with sailors, vikings, storms, a bishop's treasures and Moors just for a bit of incomplete healing?'

'You don't think God was behind it?'

'I don't know,' Galen said, unable to hide the troubled feelings that thought brought to him. 'God healed you, no doubt. But I believe the pagan Hatim healed me as far as any human could.'

'But what of God working in mysterious ways? Surely he could have engineered such a thing?'

'He could, but maybe that wasn't for my benefit. Maybe it was to reach Hatim so that he may have a positive view of Christians. Or maybe it was for the sailors or Carbo or anyone else we've come across. How can we see into His ineffable mind and know, truly know, that any event which befalls us is for our benefit or whether it benefits those around us?'

'You have been thinking deeply about this.'

'I had plenty of time to do it lying in the hospital. In a way, it is the first time since we set out on our great journey that I've had the space to think. All the rest of the time we were being held prisoner or fleeing and, it seems, travelling ceaselessly.'

'And we haven't finished that yet, either. We are only halfway. We have to get back, too.'

'I pray that will be a faster journey than this has proved to be,' Galen said. 'When do you think we can set off?'

'I've been told that the mountains aren't safe to attempt a crossing till June.'

'June!' Galen said, and he couldn't believe how dismayed he was by the news.

'I'm afraid so. It won't be time wasted though, will it? For the pope hasn't even been selected yet. Once he is enthroned, though, I should tell him, whether or not he is interested, what happened to Bishop Sigburt.'

'You'll go alone?'

'It may be for the best, but I will leave that decision to you. For the time being we have been lucky that Carbo kept his word and didn't say a thing about you and Fra' Martinus, and Lady Chedira has also kept quiet so no rumours about saints have flown around.'

'And no miracles have happened either,' Galen said, lowering his voice so that they couldn't be overheard. Not that the pilgrims could understand their Englisc, but it was best to be cautious.

'No,' Alcuin said, keeping to himself what the fra' had told him about the poisoned flour.

'That is a relief.'

'Is it really?'

'Have you ever considered what it would be like to be a saint?'

Alcuin laughed and said, 'It is unlikely to ever be attributed to me.'

'No, really, think about it. I don't mean being called a saint once you die. I mean, think about being a saint now. What are you supposed to say to people when they come to you with their problems? What sermons or words of advice should you give when they expect you to address a crowd? In what way should you live your life? How do you prevent yourself from disappointing people, especially when you can't produce miracles on cue?'

'God's Heaven, Galen, do these thoughts fill your mind?'

'Don't you think they should?'

Alcuin examined his friend's face for a minute, trying to work out what he wanted to say.

'The problem with you is you're too kind. You want to please people and make them happy. But it doesn't work out that way because other people aren't the same as you. They're selfish. They want things that benefit them and advance them and if they don't get what they want from you, they'll get angry and make a big fuss and that will hurt you.'

'I know.'

'The only way to protect yourself is to harden your heart. You need to care less about what others think and live your life as you wish, without being buffeted here and there by the whims of others.'

'I can't do that, no matter how hard I try. My only option seems to be to withdraw from the world,' Galen said, thinking it was ironic to be in this holy space that hummed with the sound of dozens of awed voices, thinking about going somewhere without any people at all.

'No! That would be terrible for you.'

'What else can I do?' Galen said. The thought of being alone made him feel very low, even for one who enjoyed being on his own.

'I don't know,' Alcuin said. 'But I'll tell you one thing. If you go off to be a recluse, I'm going with you!'

Galen laid his hand on Alcuin's arm and said, 'You would hate that even more than I would.'

'I won't let you go off on your own.'

'I really don't know why you like me so much, but I am grateful.'

'Don't be. You have earned my friendship a thousand times over. You are a good man and, what's more, you aren't a bore. I can't abide bores.'

'Like Brother Luca?'

Alcuin laughed, prompted by Galen's mischievous look that he couldn't hide.

'Brother Luca must be the laziest man I've ever met. And yes, he is a bore, for he has no interests aside from sleeping. But he's harmless.'

'Indeed. But why did you tell them of our journey?'

Galen had long wondered about that but not got around to asking until now.

'My demon of vanity, I'm afraid. I was annoyed when Feo doubted your ability to travel.'

'Well, you told a very fine tale. Had I been listening to it at my father's great hall, it would have held me spellbound.'

'Not anymore?'

'I've learned that the glamour of hardship and battle is far more pleasant to listen to beside a roaring fire than to actually deal with. Ever after this, it will colour my thoughts on any saga. The scene of us being swept from the boat was particularly affecting and would have thrilled me as a boy.'

'Aye, only now I can taste the brine in my mouth and feel the burn of it in my throat as I fought for air. I pray never to find myself in the same situation again!'

Galen nodded and his eyes swept the interior of the Pantheon, watching how the light from the great hole in the dome tracked around the vast space.

'There are other things, other parts of our journey, which I will remember with fondness. Sitting here with you in this ancient building is wonderful, but sadly not the stuff of epics.'

'It would make an excellent picture though. Those squares recessed time after time in each other form a mesmerising pattern.'

'Do you think you can reproduce that on parchment?'

'I believe I can,' Alcuin said, holding up his hand to trace what he was looking at. 'I've also experimented a bit on those visions I got from the poisonous wheat.'

'The rainbows I saw in your latest image?'

'Exactly, although the image is hard to capture in any lifelike way. I will be attempting to do something with more lively looking gargoyles next.'

'That would be interesting.'

'As interesting as the translation you did?'

'That was good. The Moorish numbering system is certainly easier than the Roman one. If it were adopted, it would make commerce far easier.'

'That isn't likely though, is it? I mean, we've used the Roman numerals for centuries.'

'Yes, but man has ever adopted easier ways of doing things, so perhaps, if the right man introduced it to people, it would get taken up.'

'The right man?'

'Not me,' Galen said, rolling his eyes. 'People wouldn't listen to me, even if I didn't dread speaking to groups. I would make a terrible preacher, you know.'

'You might not if you always preached to the same people and got to know them. I suspect you'd be alright in Hasculf's village, for instance.'

'Perhaps.'

'And you've taken a first step into joining the other monks here.'

'Not very successfully. The spit dries up in my mouth every time I try to speak.'

'It just takes practice.'

Galen nodded and said, 'I will keep trying.'

Chapter 19

I t rained so ceaselessly at the start of April that Alcuin and Galen barely left the monastery. Galen didn't dare do anything that would risk his health and getting soaked would inevitably bring down a fever. Instead, he concentrated on writing out the book about Pope Gregory, smoothing the language that was abbreviated and incomplete in places as it was a hasty transcription of the spoken word.

It was a strange document. Cardinal Gui had clearly intended to use it to flatter the pope and, by extension, the emperor, his cousin. Galen wondered whether there were any fragments of truth in the exaggerated descriptions of Gregory's wisdom and his benevolent rule.

Then he wondered if it even mattered. He shook his head - of course it did. What was the use of a biography if it wasn't truthful?

Either way, it would be a fine codex, illustrated as it was by Alcuin's images. He'd perfected his gargoyles, which crept their way up and down the edges of the pages. They had a Roman character to them and were distinctly different to anything Galen had seen of Alcuin's previous work.

'Look at that,' Brother Feo said as he stared morosely out of the scriptorium window at the downpour. 'It's too dark to work and we're missing the pope's investiture.'

'He's a Frank, you know, this Gerbert d'Aurillac,' Brother Iacopo said, joining everyone at the window, content to allow the work to cease in his scriptorium. 'Just like our abbot.'

'I wonder if they know each other?' Brother Luca said.

'Our fra' knows an awful lot of people, and they are of an age those two, so I wouldn't be surprised if they were acquainted.'

Galen, silently absorbing the conversation, was suddenly struck by an astonishing thought. He turned to Alcuin, his eyebrows raised in a question. Alcuin frowned a warning at him to say nothing, and no doubt he also wished to include an order not to think about anything, lest his face give him away.

'Does anyone know what name he is taking, this new pope of ours?' Brother Feo asked.

'I hear he will be Sylvester. Pope Sylvester the Second,' Brother Iacopo said.

Galen gave Alcuin's robe a discreet tug and as he turned round, a meaningful look, and started out of the room.

'Are you feeling unwell?' Alcuin said, then without waiting for a reply, said, 'I'll walk you to the infirmary.'

His words surprised Galen, but as Alcuin took his arm and guided him out of the room, he said nothing.

As soon as they got out of hearing range of the other monks, Galen murmured, 'I'm fine.'

'I was trying to prevent speculation from them, after you looked so struck by Fra' Martinus possibly knowing the new pope. Then you suddenly want to leave the room. It could get people thinking.'

'Oh, sorry. I didn't realise I was being so obvious.'

'I know you so well I feel like I can almost read your mind. Others probably can't, but it's best to be safe,' Alcuin said as he guided Galen into the small cloister. 'It should be safe here.'

Galen nodded and said, 'What if they do know each other? What if Fra' Martinus knew all along that Pope Gregory was going to be assassinated? Then he counselled me not to say anything, which makes me culpable too.'

'Slow down,' Alcuin said, and double-checked that they were indeed alone. 'We have no evidence that Fra' Martinus knows the new pope, much less that he knew he was plotting to be the pope. It seems to me that wrangling to be pope is so complex that nobody could guarantee getting the job even if they did plot to get it.'

'But I had a vision and I didn't do enough!' Galen said, his voice filled with anguish.

'I don't know what else you could have done. You delivered your warning to the pope himself.'

'I should have tried harder. I shouldn't have given up the moment he denied me.'

'You didn't! Galen, you tried harder than any other man might. But in the end, the pope told you he was a greater man than you. It was his choice to ignore you and he has paid the price for doing so.'

'Oh, I don't understand!' Galen cried as he clutched at his head. 'Why give me a vision of the pope being in danger and then incapacitate me almost immediately? How am I to do God's will if He makes everything so complicated?

Why can't I just see what to do and then do it? Have I failed Him by my inability, Alcuin?'

'I don't know. I don't understand it either. But if you failed God, then so did I, for all I did was take your fears to Fra' Martinus. He talked me out of going to see the pope and that, as far as I was concerned, was the end of the matter. For which I apologise. I should have tried harder.'

'We both should have.'

Alcuin nodded and subsided into thought as Galen watched, feeling more and more wretched.

'There is another explanation of what might have happened,' Alcuin said eventually.

'What explanation?'

'The devil might have tried to stop you.'

'How?' Galen said in horror.

'Maybe it was he who made you collapse outside the Lateran Palace and made the pope's visage look so sinister.'

'But if that is so, then the new pope could be in league with the devil! And if he is, and if Fra' Martinus was in the know, then he is too.'

'Let's not get carried away. There is far too much supposition in all of this.'

'You're right,' Galen said as he chewed nervously on his nail. He wasn't sure how the abbot being a non-believer might or might not play into his theory. 'I mustn't allow myself to be drawn into hysteria, although I tell you, I am precious close to it. I don't understand anything anymore and yet, once, I believed I was quite good at working things out.'

'You are good at that. You just have a bigger problem to solve than usual. Maybe we both need to give it more time.'

Galen was soothed by Alcuin's tone if not by his words. He had no choice. He had to be patient.

CHAPTER 20

Galen's questions rolled over and over in his mind like a stone in a mill, grinding away but getting nowhere. He was exhausted by the attempt to find answers. But the more angles he looked at his troubles from, the more doubt it led to.

At times during the night, he felt he might go mad if he didn't somehow stop thinking. Try as he might, though, he couldn't empty his mind or think of other things. The doubts kept plaguing him.

As the days progressed, he felt more and more exhausted. It was an agony to get out of bed and drag himself to the morning service and even the prayers and the chanting barely got through to him. He'd suddenly find himself at the end of a long choral passage with no idea of how he'd reached it or whether he'd played his part properly and carried the tune.

He didn't even care. All his befuddled brain took in was Alcuin's worried face. So he forced a smile to reassure him and drifted back to his dilemma.

'Brother Galen, the abbot wants you,' a voice said from behind as they were leaving the church.

Galen didn't even realise it had been addressed to him till the stares of the others who'd stopped to listen brought him to the realisation that he was the centre of attention.

Galen flushed bright red and said, 'What? I'm sorry?'

'Fra' Martinus wants a word,' Brother Ricardo said.

Galen froze, terrified by the possible reason for the abbot's summons.

'He'll be there in a moment,' Alcuin said as he took firm hold of Galen's arm and guided him back into motion.

'Why does he want to see me?' Galen whispered as they hurried away. 'Why now?'

'There's only one way to find out,' Alcuin said at his most tranquil. 'And I will wait outside the abbot's door so you needn't fear that you will be alone.'

Galen nodded a distracted thanks and allowed Alcuin to guide him up to the abbot's room. His breath caught in his throat as he raised his hand to knock on the door, and he couldn't prevent it from shaking.

'Come!' said the voice from the other side.

Galen gave Alcuin another agonised look, wishing his friend could go in with him, and then he stepped inside.

'Brother Galen, are you alright?' Fra' Martinus asked, looking up from the book he'd been reading. He was leaning so close to the page that it was only a hand's distance from his eyes. 'You are alarmingly pale.'

'I'm fine,' Galen said, trying to keep the tremor from his voice as he took the seat on the other side of the desk.

Fra' Martinus gave him a dubious look, readjusted the blanket covering his lap and said, 'You'd best sit before you collapse. And tell me, did you have your breakfast?'

'Yes... I think so — yes.'

'You aren't certain?'

'I had breakfast,' Galen said hastily, anxious not to upset this man, especially as breakfast was a special dispensation, to get him back to full health.

'You're very nervous.'

'No.'

'You should never lie, Brother Galen. You are terrible at it. And to deny your nerves when you sit before me trembling from head to foot makes it particularly ridiculous.'

'I'm sorry,' Galen whispered.

'Now, what have I done to instil this fear? You weren't so shaken when you visited me last. You were anxious, but nothing like this.'

Galen stared at him feeling like a trapped animal and the abbot drummed his fingers looking him over.

'Let's see, what has changed?'

'The pope,' Galen said, cursing his unruly tongue for blurting it out. But, scared as he was, he also wanted to know.

'Ah! Now I understand. He is a Frank and so am I. Was that your reasoning?'

'Did you know him?' Galen asked, clasping his hands tightly in his lap and praying the desk hid them from view.

'I knew him a long time ago. We were boys in the same monastery. But I haven't seen him in years and while I knew he had an interest in the papacy, I neither knew nor cared what he was doing about it. However, he wasn't the only candidate, and it is entirely possible that none of the candidates were involved in the death of Pope Gregory. Many of them had supporters in different camps who may have taken matters into their own hands. Or alternatively, it may have been one of the anti-pope's supporters bent on revenge. It's far too complicated to unravel.'

'I should have tried harder when I warned him!'

'He was surrounded by people protecting him. They warned him every day of the danger his life was in. I doubt they could have done anything more, even having heard your warning.'

'Then why was I sent the vision?'

Fra' Martinus paused, and Galen suspected it was because he looked desperate.

Maybe that was why the fra' spoke more kindly as he said, 'You couldn't have done more. You couldn't have changed what happened.'

'Then why?'

'You don't believe it was the wheat?'

'No,' Galen whispered.

There was no point in repeating that he'd not eaten the bread that day.

'I am told you are level-headed and I know you are an honourable man,' Fra' Martinus said. 'You have not divulged my dangerous secret, so I will tell you again and I pray you believe me. You had no hope of changing what happened to Pope Gregory. No-one in the Lateran Palace, the pope included, would have paid the least heed to what you said. They had self-proclaimed saints and prophets coming to them hourly, with all sorts of warnings. They couldn't have told you apart from any of the others.'

'And you don't believe that I am different.'

Fra' Martinus paused and examined Galen. He was panting with fear, aware of how abrupt he'd been and yet, terrified as he was, he had to ask his question.

'Do you?' Fra' Martinus asked.

'I don't know.'

'Well, I know someone who may be able to tell you.'

'You do?'

'My old friend Gerbert d'Aurillac is a renowned scholar. His interest in garnering knowledge led him to visit all the places of great learning, including Cordoba, where he learned a good deal about Moorish astronomy. He is well known for being a master of philosophy, mathematics and physical subjects. So I sent him your translation of the Moorish book on numbers and he has expressed an interest in meeting you.'

'Oh!' Galen said as a wave of fear swept over him, so powerful that it made him feel dizzy.

'You, I am afraid, have no choice in the matter. Having been summoned by the new pope, you must go. But I will tell you this: Gerbert d'Aurillac has great knowledge. If you explain all that you have experienced, he will apply his formidable brain to the problem and produce some solution. Whether it is a solution you can live with is another question entirely.'

'Oh,' Galen said again, stunned that he was going to meet a second pope.

Now, when he'd decided it was best to avoid all of them.

'You had better rest for the remainder of the day. You are expected to present yourself at the Lateran Palace tomorrow morning.'

'Yes...'

'That is all, Brother Galen. You may leave now,' Fra' Martinus said and bowed his head back over his book.

'What of Brother Alcuin?'

'He is to accompany you. I mentioned to the pope that you might require support,' the fra' said without looking up.

Galen flushed, uncertain of how to take the last comment. Then he stood and hurried to the door.

He stopped, his hand on the latch, turned and said, 'Thank you.'

'You are a very polite young man. Now go and do as I have ordered. Get some rest and get your friend to feed you.'

Galen suspected he must have looked deeply shocked as he walked out of the abbot's study and that was why Alcuin wrapped an arm about his waist and walked him only as far as the nearest bench before easing him down onto it.

'What happened?'

'Oh, Alcuin,' Galen said, turning an anguished gaze upon his friend, 'we're going to meet the pope!'

CHAPTER 21

Galen suspected he looked so nervous on the morning he was due to meet the pope that he wasn't surprised Piero and the other brothers of the scriptorium crowded around him wishing him well. They didn't know the real reason for his visit, at least that had never come out. They assumed he and Alcuin were only going to deliver the completed codex of the life of Pope Gregory V.

The abbot had suggested Galen take it with them to give to the pope who could then give it to the emperor. It was a political move so that the pope could gain favour with the emperor. But it was also helpful for Galen to have a gift to hand the pope. Galen was just grateful to have something to do, rather than only speaking to Pope Sylvester about his troubling sainthood question.

'Are you alright, Brother?' Piero asked, patting the side of his arm.

'Oh, yes, thank you for your concern,' Galen said.

'It's a great honour to meet the pope,' Brother Iacopo said as he handed over the codex, now wrapped in a fine cloth for protection. 'And you will deliver the codex as a representative of San Agato. Please remember that.'

'I will,' Galen said as he held the book propped against his chest. 'I'm sorry for taking this opportunity from you, Brother.'

'There's no need for an apology. If I were delivering the codex, it would have been to Cardinal Gui who would never have bothered to tell the pope about the craftsmen responsible for its production. It was a canny move of the fra' to get you to deliver it.'

'We will make sure the pope is fully aware of everyone behind it,' Alcuin said. 'Now we'd best be off, especially if we hope to be back by dinnertime.'

'Well, good luck with that,' Brother Luca said. 'I've heard there is always a massive queue of people to see the pope.'

'All the more reason to get a move on,' Alcuin said and guided Galen out of the scriptorium and on into the cloister where Carbo was waiting, his heavy staff in hand.

'Will that be necessary?' Galen asked, because it just added to his sense of the magnitude of the upcoming meeting which, in turn, increased his anxiety.

'No sense in letting our guard down now,' Carbo said. 'And you'd best let me take most of your weight, Brother Galen. We don't want you arriving exhausted before the pope.'

Galen was grateful for the suggestion, also because he could hardly focus. The trip out of the abbey, down the densely populated lanes of central Rome, through the wilderness of the ruined area, all the way to the Lateran Palace, passed as a barely noticed blur. At the same time, it was over too quickly and he, Carbo and Alcuin were standing in the reception hall filled with people whose voices bounced off the stone walls making a deafening cacophony.

'This queue looks to be the one to join,' Alcuin murmured.

Galen could barely manage a distracted nod as a priest walked up to them.

'What do you want?' he snapped. 'This vestibule isn't for mere monks. Look about you, can't you see the calibre of person here?'

Galen had to agree that their party looked shabby amongst the fine robes of the nobility of Rome and the scarlet gowns of a surprising number of cardinals.

'My friend has a summons from the pope,' Alcuin said as he looked the man up and down in his best imperious style.

Carbo nodded, giving the man the kind of deathly stare only possible from an ex-soldier.

At mention of the pope the man's face faltered and he said in more polite tones, 'Wait here, I'll inform his secretary.'

Alcuin nodded while Carbo shifted his grip on Galen to give him more support.

'It seems all the world is here to see the pope,' Alcuin said. 'Nobles, merchants and bishops all clamouring for something. There's such a racket I can't make out one voice from the other. If this is what this place is always like, then Fra' Martinus was right. We would never have got through to see the pope if we'd come on our own. Even if we'd arrived with Bishop Sigburt I suspect we'd have had a long wait.'

Galen gave a jerky nod as the priest who'd first spoken to them came back all agog.

'You don't happen to be Brother Galen, do you?'

'That's my friend,' Alcuin said, doing all the speaking because Galen was far too distracted. His mind was fixed entirely on the ordeal ahead.

The priest's gaze ran over Galen, obviously burning with curiosity about him, and Galen forced a rictus-like smile while he was examined.

'The pope's secretary said you were expected,' the priest said in an under voice, throbbing with awe. 'He even knew your name. That is so rare!'

'Really?' Alcuin said.

Galen was in hearty agreement with his uneasy tone. What had Fra' Martinus said to raise them to such prominence?

Fortunately, or unfortunately, Galen couldn't decide, the pope's secretary didn't keep them waiting. He turned out to be a surprisingly young man whose sombre clothes indicated that he didn't belong to a holy order and who gave them a surprisingly deep bow.

'I am Piccardo, His Holiness's secretary. Please follow me.'

Galen found Piccardo faintly reassuring. At least he was treating them in much the same way as he might treat a noble. This clearly pricked the priest's curiosity. But as it was obvious he wasn't expected to follow, he stopped at the threshold of the entrance hall and watched as Galen, Carbo and Alcuin were led deeper into the palace.

'I wish we were visiting the palace under less worrying circumstances,' Alcuin whispered into Galen's ear. 'It would be fantastic to stroll through these halls. They're filled with the greatest treasures I've ever seen and these coloured marble decorations lead the eye on from one wonder to the next.'

Galen nodded, because he knew Alcuin was just trying to distract him with the opulence of the Lateran palace. But they were moving swiftly, following the secretary who seemed blind to the marvels and merely bent on delivering them to his master.

The man stopped at an ornate set of doors that reached all the way to the ceiling, and said, 'I'm afraid only Brother Galen is allowed to go further.'

'Oh,' Alcuin said and gave Galen an apologetic shrug. 'I suppose that was to be expected.'

'The pope is in the next room,' the secretary said. 'You two may stay here at the door. Have no fear, I will look after Brother Galen.'

Galen gave Piccardo a surprised look and then a quick nod as he eased his arm out of Carbo's grip.

'I have no choice,' he murmured.

'We'll be waiting.'

'I know.'

Galen forced a brief smile which probably did nothing to hide his terror. It would have been nerve-wracking at the best of times, but after what happened with Pope Gregory, it was even worse.

Piccardo looked down at Galen who felt like an unimpressive, frail little monk and said, 'You have no reason to fear him.'

'No... of course not,' Galen said jerkily as he followed the secretary.

He was grateful for those kind words, even if the secretary had betrayed no emotion while delivering them.

They stepped into a small space entirely closed off by tapestries and Piccardo closed the door, blocking Galen's view of Alcuin and Carbo. It made his heart kick with fright. Then he took a deep breath and steeled himself. If he was ever going to prove that he was a man, a being capable of looking after himself, it was here and now.

Piccardo pushed aside the tapestry and indicated for Galen to go through. The room was surprisingly large but gloomy. All Galen could see was a series of red marble columns carved in spirals which, at the foot and the ceiling, were edged with carved gilt lacework.

Peering past the columns he saw a canopy in red and gold cloth looming over a gilded chair covered in cushions. A bored-looking, white-haired, white-bearded man in a simple gold and white robe sat there, his elbow resting on one arm, propping up his head.

Several steps below, pacing energetically up and down, was an extremely fat, well-dressed man. His red robes were so richly embroidered that they only just showed his religious calling, while his purple pockmarked face was the definition of corruption through overconsumption.

'Don't try your arguments against me, Gerbert,' the pacing man said. 'You will not convince me this is the correct path.'

'I don't have to convince you, Gui,' the pope said with an amused smile. 'I have spoken; the church will no longer tolerate simony and concubinage.'

'But think of the repercussions. Think of the difficulty of enforcement!'

'Think of your mistress?' the pope said with a sardonic twist of his lips.

'I have no mistress!' Gui growled.

The pope arched a sceptical brow as his eyes swept down to his secretary and he gave a nod of dismissal.

Piccardo bowed, then left. Galen wanted to grab on to him, to not be left alone with two of the most powerful men in the church. Instead, he hugged the codex he was carrying and sent a couple of prayers up to God to beg for protection.

The pope gave him an unimpressed look that Galen could hardly blame him for. He had seldom felt more insignificant than now. Then the pope turned back to the cardinal.

'Do you know, Gui, you should cultivate the habit of calling me Sylvester from now on, especially when we have an audience.'

'I don't understand why you took that name. The feast day for Saint Sylvester is the last day of the year. What are you trying to tell us with that? What is its symbolism?'

'I intended nothing but to reflect my admiration for a pope who built a great many of our finest churches in this city and who, moreover, managed to hold on to power for twenty-one years.'

'People claim you chose that date because it prefigures the millennium when the world may come to an end.'

'That was not my reason,' Gerbert said flatly.

'Is that all you have to say? Have your vaunted debating skills left you when all you can do is issue a denial?'

Gerbert sighed at what, to Galen, sounded like an obvious attempt to draw him into an argument. But his curiosity was also piqued. The pope was a renowned debater? It caused him to look up and his eyes met the pope's. He felt himself turn bright red and hastily looked back down at the ground.

'Much as I enjoy crossing verbal swords with you, Gui, I have other matters to attend to now.'

'The little monk?' Gui said with a dismissive toss of his head in Galen's direction. 'You would turn me out because you wish to talk to a mere monk?'

'Not a mere monk, Gui. A saint.'

His words shot a dart of fear through Galen. He hadn't expected that the pope would come out and say such a thing, as if it was a fact and not a matter for debate.

'A saint?' Gui said with a laugh. 'Well, he has the look of one, at any rate.'

'Has he?'

'You know as well as I do that the majority of living saints fall into two categories: the charismatic, robust ones that deceive people through the power of their will, like the late Marozia—'

'Ah yes, Marozia. Have we discovered who it was who betrayed her yet?'

'We have not, and I don't see why you would want to, either.'

'Because an injustice was done, Gui,' Gerbert said softly.

Galen looked up in an involuntary jerk. The pope didn't know about Gregory's role? Not only that, but he cared that she had disappeared and feared she was most likely dead?

'But don't let me divert you, Gui,' the pope continued, 'tell me of the other kind of living saint.'

'The other kind are the ones like him. Frail creatures hemmed about with minders who are the first to claim the miraculous abilities of their charges.'

'But I have it on the authority of a bishop that this boy is a saint,' Gerbert said as he held up a letter. 'And what is more, my friend Martinus, the abbot of San Agato, vouches for him and tells me of an additional miracle.'

'They are fools.'

'Possibly, but I wish to speak to this young man before I dismiss him out of hand. So, you must leave.'

'I never thought you'd use such a poor ploy to get me to leave, Gerbert. Becoming pope has sucked your wiliness away. But if you command it, I will go.'

'Ah, but I do,' the pope said with a smile that didn't reach his eyes.

Eyes that remained fixed on Gui till he had left the room. He smiled at the defiant slam of the door, then turned his attention back to Galen who glanced apprehensively up at him.

'Come closer, young man.'

Galen closed his eyes briefly to gather his strength, then, feeling light-headed with fear, he shuffled towards the dais, both arms wrapped tightly about the codex. He stopped at the bottom step, bowed low, and then looked up uncertainly.

'Come up,' the pope said.

As Galen reached the top step, the pope said, 'You can sit there.'

Galen bowed deeply, subsided onto the step and then glanced up at the pope. He was smiling in amusement, although Galen couldn't understand why. Gerbert placed his hand over Galen's head and he shook with fright at the touch.

'You have no reason to fear me, my son.'

'No, Your Holiness,' Galen whispered.

Gerbert arched a brow.

'Now... did you agree or disagree? Do you even know yourself, trembling as you are?'

Galen stared up at the pope, uncertain what he should say. He felt as tongue-tied before this man as he had when standing before his father as a boy.

'I believe you have many things to tell me. Let us start with what happened to your bishop, for in his letter his intention was to present himself in Rome.'

'He did set off. But we were shipwrecked and then captured by the Moors. They... they tortured Bishop Sigbert to death.'

'So he was martyred,' the pope said, then paused at the glance Galen flicked up at him.

Galen feared his face gave his uncertainty away.

'He wasn't martyred?' the pope asked.

'Bishop Sigbert was bringing two treasures to Rome. It became common knowledge in Lundenburh. From there, the vikings found out about it and set an ambush, which was why we were shipwrecked, as were the vikings. A group of raiding Moors came upon the vikings first and so, too, learned of the treasure and came to find us. The first... the first treasure was easy enough to find. It was in a chained and padlocked chest.'

'And what was this treasure that the Moors cheated me of?'

'A great cross of gold. It was very beautiful.'

'Ah, a significant loss indeed. And yet, you interest me, for the cross seemed to hold value to you only as a thing of beauty. The fact that it was made of gold and most likely worth a king's ransom appears not to worry you at all.'

'Oh, um,' Galen said, unsure whether he was being praised or criticised and what to add.

'And the second treasure?' the pope asked.

Galen was relieved to move on without coming up with an explanation, although it was true - for him the true value of the cross was its beauty.

'Well... the Moors couldn't find it, and that was why they tortured the bishop. He refused to give it up, and it was strange, for they searched the chest and all the sailors and soldiers and me and Alcuin.'

'Alcuin?'

'My brother monk,' Galen said as he glanced up, caught the pope's eye and hastily looked away.

'This Brother Alcuin travelled with you too?'

'Yes...' Galen took a deep breath and said, 'He came to look after me.'

'I see. Well, continue with your tale, for it does actually interest me.'

'The Moors set to torturing Bishop Sigbert so that he would give up the second treasure, but he was steadfast in his refusal. Till... till the wounds he'd sustained grew too great and everyone knew he'd die. Then the Moors carried him into one of their great halls and brought me and Alcuin in to see him. We didn't realise it at the time, but... they were listening in to everything the bishop said. And I... I had made that easier, for I had taught one of their number to speak Englisc.'

'I see. We will come back to that. What happened next?'

'Well,' Galen said and paused as the next bit was embarrassing, 'with his last breath, Bishop Sigbert told us that... that I was the second treasure, because... because he thought me a saint.'

Galen raised a deeply flushed face, embarrassed to have confessed such a thing, and was surprised to find that the pope looked amused.

'I see. So he was tortured to reveal a treasure and because at the eleventh hour he let down his guard and betrayed you, you don't think he was martyred?'

'No. I just wonder if being tortured to death to protect a treasure can be classed as martyrdom. His faith wasn't being tested. They didn't ask him to renounce God. They were just trying to get their hands on a material good and he was adamant that they wouldn't.'

'But my dear young man, that material good was you.'

'It doesn't matter what it was,' Galen said, his eyes fixed on the marble floor. 'It had nothing to do with his faith.'

'Perhaps it had everything to do with his faith if he truly believed he was keeping a saint out of the hands of the Moors. What greater service could he do for God?'

'But he was willing to allow all the sailors and soldiers to be killed to protect his secret, too.'

'He was?'

'When the Moors first came upon us, they threatened to kill each man, one by one, until the bishop told them where he'd hidden the treasures.'

'He believed he was doing the right thing, preserving your life at the cost of all those others,' Gerbert said, and now he sounded quite gentle. 'Ah, don't clam up now. Overcome your shyness, for I am enjoying this discussion. Nothing pleases me more than to tease out the minutiae of theology and you have brought me an interesting question. It's as delightful as it was unexpected.'

Galen didn't know what more to do than give an uncertain shrug.

'Do you believe there was a different motive?' the pope asked as he slipped into a fatherly manner.

'Glory,' Galen whispered.

'Glory?'

Galen swallowed hard, uncertain he should be saying any of this, but the question had burned in his mind for such a long time and he had to have an answer. And who but the pope could give him the definitive line?

'What would he gain if he arrived in Rome with nothing to give the pope? He would have been insignificant.'

'But you say he was dying? What did he have to gain from keeping the secret even then?'

'He was losing the ultimate prize of life. There was no more motive to give in at that point and he'd already got a promise from Alcuin to take word of his demise... his martyrdom, to Rome, and to get me here... alive or dead.'

'I see,' Gerbert said. 'People's vanity is endlessly fascinating. And so you don't believe him to be a martyr?'

'It is not for me to decide.'

'Indeed not, and for reasons of politics, and because people love a good story, the tale of a bishop who was tortured to death to save the life of a saint from the infidels will work very well.'

'Only if he really was protecting a saint,' Galen whispered.

'And you don't believe he was?'

'I don't feel like a saint!'

Gerbert paused, examining Galen again as he took a deep, shuddering breath to calm himself. He'd tried hard to stifle it, but his words sounded like a cry for help.

'Bishop Sigburt wrote of three highly convincing miracles, one which so stunned him he sent word of it in a second letter just to tell my predecessor of the miracle of Christmas Eve. And Fra' Martinus, not a man to give credence to much, spoke of another miracle and a highly significant dream. All of which, young man, elevates you to a level of extreme sainthood, for many a saint has been credited with only one miracle in their whole life.'

'But I didn't feel anything,' Galen said miserably as he stared at the pope's red-clad feet.

'But you saw something, didn't you? We can discount the healing of the girl as I gather you were in no state to remember it. But you saw a man who believed that at your touch his rib had been healed. You saw a man whose breath failed him and brought him low when he came to kill you and you saw your friend, fatally injured, restored to life. Can you deny any of that?'

'No,' Galen said in a low voice as he wrapped his arms even tighter about himself.

'So why do you fear it, my son?'

'Wouldn't you?' Galen said, looking up into the pope's face and fighting against tears. 'I don't deserve adulation. I find it difficult to stand up to people and... and I have no control over these miracles. They either happen or they don't. What if... what if people want more? What if they want a miracle whenever they come to me? I can't do that. I can't even solve my own problems. How can I solve theirs?'

'My dear young man, what choice do you imagine you have in the matter?'

'What?'

This down-to-earth question quenched the hysteria Galen was teetering on the edge of.

'You are called a saint already and no amount of protestation from you, or even from me, will change anything.'

'But if people aren't encouraged, if you deny it, and nobody speaks of it, surely—'

'No,' the pope said. 'Word of your deeds is already abroad. Lundenburh is obviously rife with it and Rome will be shortly, too. No man can keep a secret such as yours. Your miracles are already being whispered about in my palace. It won't take long for them to get further.

'Whilst it might take a little longer for people to recognise you as the face behind the rumours of a new saint, in time they will know that, too. Besides, your argument presupposes that you won't perform another miracle. But I ask you, young man, what if you do?

'What if everyone in this palace sees you perform something extraordinary? Then you will be back where you started. No. I see no point in denial. It's a waste of time.'

'Then what must I do?' Galen asked.

The pope's words rang too true for him to refute them.

'First, you tell me your story, from the very beginning, right from the day you were born.'

'Why?' Galen said, so startled by the order that he looked up in astonishment.

'For no other reason than that I am your pope and I order it.'

Galen started off hesitantly. He was certain a learned and brilliant man like the pope, one who had travelled widely, would find nothing of interest in Galen's tale of his narrowly circumscribed life. But as he had no choice, he spoke as quickly as he could so as not to prolong the boredom for the pope and so that he could get over the difficult bits as swiftly as possible.

It wasn't fast enough. The pope's eyebrows rose, and he said, 'You were raped?'

Galen gave a quick nod and shuddered just to think of it.

'Very well, continue, but leave nothing out,' Gerbert said as he gazed at his storyteller, his face growing more thoughtful as the tale unfolded.

Galen hurried on, but, mindful of his instructions, left nothing out until he got to the bit with Marozia where he merely said that they had travelled a way with her.

'Fascinating,' Pope Sylvester said when Galen finally came to the end of his story. 'I must say you have exceeded my expectations. You are very matter of fact. I'd expected a little more bragging, a little more highlighting of the miracles, some dwelling on the detail. But you spoke of the miracles as you spoke of the rest of your life, a step-by-step progression where one event, fair or foul, followed the other in a strictly logical order. I like the way you order your thoughts and don't skip back and forth or embroider.'

Galen felt his face grow warm at this over-the-top praise from such a powerful man.

'You did give yourself away, though,' the pope said.

'I... I did?' Galen said, his mind racing to work out what he had said that could possibly be misconstrued.

'It was clear to me that people are the most important part of your tale. Your love of your mother, your difficult relationship with your father, and the obviously close attachment you have to this Alcuin, all shone through. And that wasn't all. Anyone who touches your life, who shows you the least bit of interest, is loved unquestioningly in return, from the villagers to the king's man, to the ship's captain to the Moor, the big monk, Carbo, and Marozia. Their rank seems to hold no interest to you, but their actions towards you were all appreciated.'

'Oh... I suppose that's true,' Galen said, embarrassed that the pope had understood him so well.

Perhaps this was a good thing, for it meant Galen could rely upon his judgement.

'Not that I think you are a holy fool, mind you. You understand that people are motivated by different things to you. You just seem incapable of keeping them at arm's length, even knowing they might be dangerous. Maybe that is what makes you a saint.'

Galen gave a non-committal shrug. It seemed the pope had already made up his mind about him.

'So anyway, that's how I came to be here.'

'You have left out one salient fact.'

'I have?' Galen said, flushing to his ear tips.

'You haven't mentioned your vision or your meeting with Pope Gregory, nor the connection you made over his death and me.'

'Oh!' Galen said, appalled that the pope knew of his suspicions. 'Did Fra' Martinus... did the fra' tell you?'

'He did. I can assure you, my young friend, that I had nothing to do with Pope Gregory's death.'

'Of course,' Galen murmured, horrified to have been so exposed.

'No 'of course' about it,' Pope Sylvester said with an amused smile. 'But I will leave you to think about what I have said and then judge for yourself in your own time. In the meantime, you can tell me about Marozia. I find it interesting that you met her.'

'We were all on the road to Rome. We fell in with her band,' Galen said, aware that he could fill the pope in on all that had happened to the woman that apparently remained a mystery to the rest of the world. It seemed her family hadn't let it be known yet, either. He was loath to divulge it without finding out why from them first.

'Did she perform a miracle when you were with her?'

'No,' Galen said and felt his face grow warm again.

'You wanted her to heal you?'

'I hoped... but it wasn't to be.'

'So you thought she might?'

Galen shrugged.

'She seemed so certain and I... I have seen others healed, so... I hoped.'

'Hope is a curious thing, is it not?' Pope Sylvester said, almost to himself. 'It hangs grimly on when all reason should have told it to give in and go away.' Galen nodded silent agreement, which earned him another smile from the pope who said, 'Do you know what happened to her?'

Galen felt trapped, transfixed by the pope's mild gaze, his blue eyes that seemed so innocent, even when the question wasn't. Omission was one thing, but lying outright, to the pope especially, was something else.

'She and her entire band were murdered and their bodies spirited away.'

The pope actually blinked at Galen and, for the first time, looked surprised.

'You saw that?'

'My companions and I barely got away with our lives.'

'Do you know who was responsible?'

This was information Galen was fine about giving out.

'Pope Gregory ordered it. He confessed to it himself when we met at the basilica.'

'Good Lord! And you've been sitting on this information all this time?'

'I told the Theophylacti, and one of their number was also present when the pope confessed.'

'Were they now?' The pope sighed and said, 'Yet another depressing lesson, young man. When you are powerful, you must always beware those around you.'

'Alcuin says that to me all the time,' Galen said with an embarrassed smile. 'He says I'm too trusting.'

'He is probably right. I recommend you always keep him near you. It sounds like he has rescued you on many an occasion.'

'I will always be grateful to him. But no man should be so bound to another as Alcuin is forced to be to me. I stifle him and prevent him from leading his own life, for he is always looking after mine. In that I am guilty of the grossest selfishness.'

'I am surprised by your passion and your powerful sense of what is right and wrong. As well as your sense of the debt you owe your friend. You did save his life. Some may say that what remains of it belongs to you.'

'God saved his life, not me. All I did was pray and beg and plead, nothing more. No more than I have done a hundred times for others.'

'And been ignored, hmmm?'

'Yes,' Galen muttered, and his eyes slipped away from the pope's penetrating gaze.

The pope watched him for a moment, and Galen guessed he must cut a strange, restless, hunched-up figure, as if his body reflected the workings of his mind and the uncertainty which pervaded his thoughts.

'You have many questions that remain unanswered,' the pope said, finally. 'I will help you discover the answers.'

'You will?'

'I have come across many people who call themselves saints in my time, most of whom fitted into the categories of bold or frail that Cardinal Gui referred to. And, in my youth, I sought such people out and questioned them, trying to discover what kind of beings they really were. And I watched them, waiting to see a miracle. I never did.

'But in my questioning of you and your life, I have found a couple of differences to those others. They all claimed the ability to bring about a miracle; you don't. They all believed themselves saints; some even claimed God had told them of their holy calling. Again, you don't. You doubt yourself. I find that interesting.'

'Maybe I am deluded,' Galen said. 'Or... or the miracles around me have been brought about by... by a power other than God's.'

'You must be speaking of the devil. No other power would be great enough.'

Galen shrugged, certain his fear and unhappiness were etched on his face.

'How else could I explain my confusion? Surely if God was the agent of the miracles, I would know. Surely if He sent me the vision warning of the danger to Pope Gregory, I would have been able to deliver it and change his fate.'

'It is a strange demon indeed, though, who would cause so many miracles of healing and salvation. Far more likely for the devil to cause things to shrivel up and die than to cast a miracle which causes people to praise God.'

'Yes,' Galen said as he went back to staring at the floor.

'You have thought of that too, hmmm?' the pope said. 'You truly are a delight. I'll tell you something, Galen - you are bound to hear of it soon enough, so I may as well be the one to do the telling. Since I was a young man, I have venerated learning only a little less than I venerate God. For that reason, I travelled far and wide, studying in the greatest monasteries, and even for a while in the libraries of Cordoba. Although sadly Cordoba is far more difficult for us to access nowadays.'

'Yes,' Galen murmured.

'There was a time when the Moors were more open. When they allowed each man to follow his own religion in his own way. It is not necessarily a wise thing to do and certainly not something I would encourage. Man should be shown the one true way. But I digress. For the purposes of my studies, it suited me well enough.

'During my stay in Cordoba, I learned many things. Through their conquests, the Moors have come across the writings of the ancients, the Greeks and the Romans, and they have translated them into their own language. I, in my turn, translated them into Latin.'

'You did?' Galen said, too surprised to curb his tongue.

Gerbert grinned and said, 'I thought that might interest you. It was Fra' Martinus sending me your translation of the Moorish book of numbers that piqued my curiosity, not the tales of the miracles. I usually leave sorting out saints to my cardinals.'

'Oh!'

'Indeed. That brings me back to the point of my tale. I, too, learned about Moorish numbers in Cordoba. As you'll know, using the Moorish numbers it is possible to calculate complex arithmetic in your head without having to write anything down.'

'Yes, I have found it so.'

'Have you demonstrated this feat to anyone?'

'No, Alcuin isn't interested in numbers.'

'Don't. My ability with numbers has led people to say that I'm a sorcerer in league with the devil.'

Galen blinked in surprise at Gerbert and felt dizziness overwhelm him. He hastily put out a hand to steady himself against the floor.

'I have shocked you,' Pope Sylvester said. 'But I give you my word before God. My abilities are purely from my book learning and nowhere else. I have no secret liaison with demons.'

'No, of course not,' Galen murmured.

'And neither have you.'

'Do you... do you think so?'

'I know it,' the pope said firmly.

Galen nodded, but he wasn't completely reassured. Even now, when he had the definitive assessment from the pope, he was uncertain. At that moment, Piccardo reappeared and respectfully cleared his throat.

'The delegation from Constantinople is here to see you, Your Holiness.'

'Ah, good. Brother Galen, you must excuse me now, but we will resume this discussion. In the meantime,

Piccardo will provide you and Brother Alcuin with accommodation.'

'He — here?' Galen said hesitantly.

'Of course. I wish to have you under my eye. Piccardo, ask Brother Alcuin in to help Brother Galen to their new quarters.'

'But the abbey?' Galen said frantically, as terror took over.

He wasn't sure he could live in such an intimidating palace. It also occurred to him that the pope had little intention of letting him go, and he wondered whether he'd ever see his home again.

'Fra' Martinus didn't expect to see you back, although, naturally, you may return to collect your belongings.'

Galen was prevented from saying anything further by the arrival of Alcuin who bowed low at the foot of the stairs leading to the pope's throne.

The pope looked surprised and then curious to see Alcuin. Galen supposed it was to be expected. Alcuin was tall and blond and could easily have passed for an angel with his deep blue eyes if it weren't for the tonsure and the monk's habit. With his looks and his air of assurance he could so easily take on the mantle of a saint.

'Welcome, Brother Alcuin,' the pope said. 'Brother Galen has told me a great deal about you.'

Alcuin flushed and said, 'Brother Galen is far too uncritical, Your Holiness. I'm sure he exaggerated my role.'

'Not at all,' the pope said. 'Now I suggest you help your friend down the stairs. I imagine our meeting has been a tiring one for him. Piccardo will show you to your new quarters.'

Alcuin's face showed a flash of query, then he hurried up the stairs, took Galen's arm and, with a well-practised move, helped him to his feet and led him down the stairs.

The pope hadn't been mistaken. His meeting had tired Galen and he was leaning heavily on his friend's arm. Alcuin turned the two of them around so that they were facing the pope. They gave a deep bow and then followed Piccardo out.

'Oh, wait, the codex!' Galen said and turned back. 'It was produced by the Abbey of San Agato, from notes sent to us by Cardinal Gui. Fra' Martinus asked me to give it to you.'

Pope Sylvester waved for Piccardo to take the book, so all that was left was for Galen to give another bow and leave. He supposed the pope had answered his key question. His Holiness thought him a saint. But where did that leave him and Alcuin now?

Enjoyed this book? You can make a huge difference
If you are like me, you use reviews to decide whether you want to buy a book. So if you enjoyed the book please take a moment to let people know why. The review can be as short as you like.
Thank you very much!
https://www.amazon.com/review/create-review

GET ALL MY SHORT STORIES FOR FREE!

Building a relationship with my readers is one of the great things about being a writer. That is why I continue to upload a wide collection of short stories for free on my website. These currently include a collection of short stories, and some individual longer short stories including a Galen spin off, a quirky tale about a rabbit in Lisbon and a couple of Christmas romances.

Sign up for my no-spam newsletter that only goes out when there is a new book or freebie available, at: www.marinapacheco.me

ALSO BY

Get all my books here:

MEDIEVAL HISTORICAL FICTION ePub, paperback and hardback
Fraternity of Brothers, *Life of Galen, Book 1* – Cast out for a crime committed against him, his future looks bleak. Until an unexpected visitor gives him hope for justice. A fight for acceptance, absolution and friendship in Anglo-Saxon England.
Comfort of Home, *Life of Galen, Book 2* – Proven innocent, he's returned from exile. Can he recover all that he lost? A tale of friendship and return to a family he thought he'd lost, set in Anglo-Saxon England.
Kindness of Strangers, *Life of Galen, Book 3* – Trapped in a land plagued by vikings, can one small miracle be all they need to survive? A tale of miracles, betrayal and friendship while under viking siege.
The King's Hall, *Life of Galen, Book 4* – As if

being commissioned to create a book to turn back the Apocalypse isn't enough, intrigue and romance threaten to destroy everything he's come to rely upon. Friendship, love and intrigue at the court of King Aethelred the Unready.

Restless Sea, *Life of Galen, Book 5* – Just when they thought they could go home, they're thrust into an adventure at sea. A journey that tests the bonds of friendship.

Friend of My Enemy, *Life of Galen, Book 6* – Captured by an implacable enemy, their future looks bleak. Will escape even be possible?

Road to Rome, *Life of Galen, Book 7* — A journey across a turbulent continent. Will Galen find the answers he seeks?

Eternal City, *Life of Galen, Book 8* — Galen and Alcuin delve into the secrets of the corrupt and decaying city of Medieval Rome.

AUDIOBOOKS narrated by Jacob Daniels
Fraternity of Brothers, *Life of Galen, Book 1*
Comfort of Home, *Life of Galen, Book 2*
Kindness of Strangers, *Life of Galen, Book 3*
The King's Hall, *Life of Galen, Book 4*
   Restless Sea, *Life of Galen, Book 5*

HISTORICAL ROMANCE: ePub, paperback, hardback and audiobooks with AI narration
Sanctuary, *a sweet Medieval mystery* – He needs shelter.

She wants a way out. Will his brave move to protect risk both their hearts? An optimistic tale of redemption with heart-warming characters and feel-good thrills.

The Duke's Heart, *a sweet Victorian romance* – His body may be weak, but his dreams know no bounds. Will she be the answer to his prayers? A disabled duke, a strong and determined woman and a slow-building relationship.

Duchess in Flight, *a swashbuckling romance* – She's on the run from a deadly enemy. He lives in the shadows of truth. When their lives merge, will their battle for survival lead to love? A reluctant hero, a woman and her children in distress, a chase to the death.

What the Pauper Did, *a body swap mystery romance* – How do you define yourself? Is it through your appearance, your memories or your soul? Intrigue, murder and romance in an alternate Lisbon of 1770.

CONTEMPORARY ROMANCE ePub, paperback, hardback and audiobooks with AI narration

Scent of Love – Can two polar opposite perfumers overcome their differences and create a unique blend all of their own? Love, intrigue and clashing values in the perfume houses of Lisbon.

Sky Therapy — A detective and the son of a serial killer. Is it safest to stay apart, or will they risk everything for love?

SCIENCE FICTION/ FANTASY ePub and paperback

City of Night, *Eternal City, Book 1* – World-threatening danger, a female demonologist, an unwitting apprentice, a city in a single tower, a satisfying ending.

SHORT STORIES: ePub, paperback, and AI narration

Living, Loving, Longing, Lisbon, Vol 1 & Vol 2 – A collection of short stories inspired by the city of Lisbon, written by people from around the world who live in, visited or love Lisbon.

Loves of Lisbon – An advent calendar of 24 short, sweet romances of the intertwining lives of the residents of Lisbon.

FREEBIES: ePub and AI narration

Shorties – My shortest works: futuristic, contemporary and historical.

White Rabbit of Lisbon – A whimsical short story. What will happen when a rabbit and a raven fall in love?

Scourge of Demons – How would you deal with your demons? A short story set in the world of the Life of Galen series.

The Greek Gift – A Christmas short story. At the gym he

ignored her; will it be any different at the Christmas Eve party?

Christmas Fates – A Christmas short story. Aurora Dawn is about to learn the true meaning of Christmas and it has nothing to do with how many of the latest must-haves she can sell.

ABOUT AUTHOr

Marina Pacheco a binge writer of historical fiction, sweet romance, sci-fi and fantasy novels as well as short stories. She writes easy reading, feel-good novels that are perfect for a commute or to curl up with on a rainy day. She currently lives on the coast just outside Lisbon, after stints in London, Johannesburg, and Bangkok, which all sounds more glamorous than it actually was. Her ambition is to publish 100 books. This is taking considerably longer than she'd anticipated!

You can find out more about Marina Pacheco's work, and download several freebies, on her website: https://marinapacheco.me
Website: https://marinapacheco.me
   Sign up to Marina's newsletter via her website or on Substack to keep up to date on all her writing activities, get early previews of covers and first chapters, short stories and freebies.
Follow me on substack:
https://substack.com/@marinapacheco
email: hi@marinapacheco.me

Printed in Great Britain
by Amazon

61741461R00129